THE CASE of the LOST LOOKALIKE

Other Avon Camelot Books by
Carol Farley

THE CASE OF THE VANISHING VILLAIN
MYSTERY IN THE RAVINE
MYSTERY OF THE FOG MAN
MYSTERY OF THE MELTED DIAMONDS

CAROL FARLEY is the author of many popular books for young readers, including *Mystery in the Ravine*, *Mystery of the Fog Man*, *Mystery of the Melted Diamonds*, and the first Flee Jay and Clarice adventure, *The Case of the Vanishing Villain*, all Avon Camelot books.

Carol Farley lives in a cottage by a lake with an island. No exciting mysteries have ever really happened there, but she says a vivid imagination can work magic. She and her family have lived in Michigan for many years.

THE CASE of the LOST LOOKALIKE

CAROL FARLEY

Illustrated by Tom Newsom

THE CASE OF THE LOST LOOKALIKE is an original publication of Avon Books. This work has never before appeared in book form.

AVON BOOKS
A division of
The Hearst Corporation
105 Madison Avenue
New York, New York 10016

Published by arrangement with the author
Library of Congress Catalog Card Number: 87-27070
ISBN: 0-380-75450-9
RL: 5.2

Library of Congress Cataloging-in-Publication Data:

Farley, Carol.
The case of the lost lookalike.

(An Avon Camelot book)
Summary: While spending part of the summer at picturesque Magic Lake, twelve-year-old Flee Jay and her competitive bright younger sister become involved with a hermit, vandalism, and a forty-year-old mystery concerning a kidnapped child.
[1. Sisters—Fiction. 2. Mystery and detective stories] I. Newsom, Tom, ill. II. Title.
PZ7.F233Car 1988 [Fic] 87-27070

First Avon Camelot Printing: January 1988

Printed in the U.S.A.

OPM 10 9 8 7 6 5 4 3 2 1

This book is dedicated to
Carol Beach York—
good friend
and terrific writer!

Contents

The Invitation

It all started in May when Aunt Doris and I were sitting in the kitchen talking. She had just come to visit for a weekend. Mom and Dad weren't home from work yet, and Clarice wasn't home from the library, so we were having a snack while we waited. Snacking and laughing are the things we do best together.

Aunt Doris reached for another cookie. It was her fourth one, but who was counting? "I'm going to Magic Lake for my vacation again this year, Flee Jay," she said. "Want to go along with me?"

I bolted forward so fast I nearly spilled my hot chocolate. "My gosh, yes!" Right that second I couldn't think of anything better.

"I'm going to rent a cottage right near the lake, the way I did last year," she went on. "We can sunbathe and swim all day long."

I looked at the pile of cookie crumbs in front of me and sighed. Imagining myself in a bathing suit wasn't all that thrilling. I don't have to shop in those queen-size stores yet, but my hips were definitely getting a little royal. "Guess I'd better get busy with a diet, then."

"You worry too much about how you look, honey." Aunt Doris gestured to her own body, which was even more queenly than my own. "I figure my weight is just right for my height." She laughed. "As soon as I grow about five more inches."

I had to laugh then, too. Aunt Doris and I spend a lot of time giggling when we're together. Mom says the two of us are a lot alike, so maybe that's why we get along so well. We even look alike. My hair is a rusty color and it's naturally frizzy, and so is Aunt Doris's. We both have freckles and round faces and the same color eyes. The funny thing is that on Aunt Doris my looks are just fine. It's only on me that they seem pitiful.

"Magic Lake isn't a big resort area yet," Aunt Doris went on, walking over to the sink to wash out her cup, "because it's so isolated people don't know about it. But it's beautiful up there."

I had to smile as she wiped the cup and put it away. In her own apartment, Aunt Doris lets dishes pile up until they nearly walk away by themselves. But when she visits us, she tries to be like Mom, the second-place winner in the World's Neatest Person Contest.

Clarice, my ten-year-old sister, is the first-place winner. She would win first place in almost any contest you could think of, in fact. Clarice is gorgeous and has the IQ of a genius. She's a walking, talking world almanac. I'm nearly three years older than she is, but she's the brain in our family. Clarice absorbs facts the way I absorb calories.

Most of the time I don't mind that she's so smart. After all, I've got a sense of humor, and Clarice doesn't. I figure that a good laugh is better than a bunch of useless facts any old day. So normally I just smile while Clarice pontificates on complicated subjects.

"There's a bit of a mystery surrounding the people who live there all year long," Aunt Doris said, sitting down again.

"Really?" I could feel my ears perk up the same way my

dog Ginger's do when the mailman's getting close. You see, I want to be a famous detective one day, and if I ever have the chance to solve a case without Clarice, I'll know I have the right kind of brain. I want to swoop in and spout out the answers to baffling mysteries while everyone around me blinks in befuddlement. I want to reveal the amazing solutions to puzzles while everyone gasps in admiration. Except the criminal, of course, who gasps for other reasons.

But so far I haven't had a chance to work alone. In the only mystery we've run into, Clarice was the one swooping in while I stood there blinking like a digital clock in a power outage. The thing is, though, that I know she could never come up with the right solutions without me helping her. I think there's more to solving mysteries than just accumulating a bunch of facts. Without her at Magic Lake, maybe I could—

"I'm sure Clarice will want to hear all about it, too," Aunt Doris said, breaking into my thoughts.

I sagged back against my chair. "Are you going to ask Clarice to go, too?"

"Well, of course I want to ask her, Flee Jay! She likes swimming, doesn't she?"

"Not if she has to get dirty. You know how Clarice feels about germs, Aunt Doris. She swims in chlorinated pools, where everything is super clean. Don't fish go to the bathroom in Magic Lake?"

Aunt Doris laughed. "Well, I never asked one, but I guess so."

"Then maybe Clarice won't want to go."

"Go where?"

Clarice came hurrying into the kitchen, her ugly black purse strung over her shoulder. She says she bought it in a yard sale for a dime, but if you ask me, I think the lady having the sale paid Clarice the dime to take it away. On the inside the purse is filled with pencils and notebooks Clarice has crammed with facts, and on the outside it has a layer of rhinestones big enough to choke a horse. We don't have purse snatchers in Grand Channel, Michigan, but even if we did, Clarice's would be safe.

"Where won't I want to go?" she asked, getting a bag of alfalfa sprouts out of the fridge. Her snacks have to be more nourishing than cookies are.

"I'm going up to Magic Lake again this August," Aunt Doris told her. "And I wondered if you girls might like to go along for a few days' vacation."

Clarice tapped her finger against her chin. "Is there a good library there?"

Aunt Doris thought a moment. "I don't think so. You can buy a few magazines at the general store, I guess. Although last year it seemed to me that the most sales in that store were for lottery tickets. Everyone up there must have been hoping to win a big jackpot. But, no, I don't think there's a library, honey. Can't you live without one for a week?"

Clarice blinked her big blue eyes. "I'm not sure. I've never tried."

Aunt Doris winked at her. "It might be a novel idea for you, then. You could learn how to be booked up even without a library."

"I'll page you if you're needed, Clarice," I said, jumping into the fun. "I'll cover for you if you need a jacket. It can be a whole new chapter in your life."

Aunt Doris shrieked with laughter. "That's good, Flee Jay. That's good!"

"What's good?" Clarice asked. "What so funny?"

At the end of five minutes, she still hadn't seen anything to laugh about, but she finally did agree to go to Magic Lake with Aunt Doris and me. "Magic Lake is fed by underground springs," she said, "so it's one of the cleanest lakes in Michigan. It ought to be okay for swimming."

I put my cup in the sink. "Well, I don't care about that. I'm going to get all suntanned and beautiful. I hate to be seen in a bathing suit around here. Too many boys."

"Oh, there aren't many up there," Aunt Doris assured me. "Magic Lake is rather deserted. And kind of eerie, too, at times. There's that mystery I mentioned earlier."

Clarice's eyebrows shot up. "A mystery! Maybe I can solve it!"

"You?" I glared at her. "What about me? I may not get all the answers, but you can't solve a mystery without me."

And then she said the words I most dread to hear. "Nanny, nanny, boo, boo," she called, whirling around and flaring out her pink dress. "You can't do what I do!"

"I can too! I—"

"Oh my goodness, girls," Aunt Doris blurted before I could say any more. "This mystery isn't one that you can solve. It's just something strange that happened years and years ago, that's all. I'm sorry I brought it up, and I'm not going to talk about it again. There isn't anything there to solve, and that's that! Come on, now, let's start making some plans. You're going to have a ball when we get to Magic Lake!"

But as it turned out, Aunt Doris was wrong, and this is what I want to tell you about. Oh, we had a good time at the lake all right, and I got tanned even though I didn't get beautiful. But she was wrong about the mystery. We did solve it. And believe it or not, *I* was the one who came up with the most important clue.

Clarice, in her usual modest manner, says that she could have done it all on her own.

So that's why I want to write it all down. I want to show you exactly what happened. Then you can tell me what you think. Should Clarice get credit for solving *The Case of the Lost Lookalike*, or should I?

The Mysterious Hermit

It was only a three-hour drive to Magic Lake, but it seemed a lot longer because of Clarice. She sat in the front seat reading a book from the Grand Channel Library and scribbling into her notebooks. Every now and then she would hang over the seat to announce another one of her useless facts. They buzzed around us like flies, and to me they were just as annoying.

"Zippers were invented in 1910," she declared after a pleasant but too-short silence. "The Duke of Windsor was the first one to have one in his pants."

Aunt Doris tried to look interested, but I only groaned. Finally, in order to keep Clarice quiet, I begged Aunt Doris to tell us about the mystery she had hinted at weeks before.

"Promise you won't fight if I do? I mean it, girls. I'm not going to put up with arguing about who's the great detective the way you were doing back home. There's nothing to solve here. It's just a strange story about a strange old man, that's all. So there's no point in fighting. When you two go at it tooth and nail, I can't even think straight."

Clarice's head bobbed over into the backseat again. Her long blonde hair smelled like the disinfectant she uses to wash her combs and brushes. "Do you know why people use that expression? It's because pirates used to hide sharp nails in their mouths and . . ."

My glare silenced her. "We're not going to fight," I told Aunt Doris.

"We don't really fight anyway," Clarice chimed in. "We just compare ideas."

Aunt Doris nearly drove the car off the road. "That's the world's biggest understatement," she said, "but I might as well tell you the little bit I know about the old story. You'll be seeing Merkin Island, and you'll wonder about it once we get there."

She took a deep breath. "Actually I don't know the details of what happened to the Merkin family. Mrs. Quist—she's the woman who owns the rental cottages—is a bit of a gossip. She flitted in and out last summer telling me bits and pieces of the story. She never stayed long enough to tell the whole thing because she was busy supervising the work on some more cottages she was having built. She was worrying about the cost, so she made sure the carpenters worked every minute that she was paying them for.

"Anyway, she told me that at one time all the lake area belonged to a family named Merkin. Evidently they slowly sold away all the lots on the shore, but they kept the island out in the middle of the lake for themselves. They built a huge estate out there. As the years passed, only one man was left—Ezra Merkin. He married a young woman, and they had a child. But something terrible happened, and the mother and daughter both died. I'm not entirely clear on how they died, but it must have been pretty bad, because Ezra Merkin became more and more of a recluse. Mrs. Quist told me he's lived like a hermit on that island for years now, never leaving and never allowing any visitors. That's the mystery I was talking about. It seems terribly sad to me. I wonder how he can stand the loneliness."

Sighing, she shook her head. "Last summer I thought

about him every time I looked out my cottage window late at night. I could see the lights blinking on that island, and I would get an eerie feeling. It gives me the creeps to think somebody is living like a hermit all hidden away like that, no family, no friends."

It gave me the creeps, too. I couldn't imagine how lonely it would be not to have family, never to see friends. Clarice drives me bonkers—everybody knows that—but life without her would be pretty dull. And having Mom and Dad around is kind of like having a two-member cheering squad on my side no matter what game I'm playing. And if I didn't have friends, I think I'd just shrivel up and wither away. I need them as much as I need hamburgers and french fries. And that's a lot!

Clarice was thinking of more practical problems. "How can he get food and things?"

"Oh, he has lots of money. He hires servants. And pays them fairly well, according to Mrs. Quist. But they have to agree to live on the island without having visitors. They can go to the shore in boats in the summer or on snowmobiles in the winter, but sometimes in the spring and the fall, when the lake is beginning to thaw or freeze, they can't go anywhere."

I thought of all the fun I had going to shopping malls and wandering around Channel Point with my friends. "I could never do it," I said.

"Others feel the same, I guess," Aunt Doris agreed. "When I left last summer, Mrs. Quist was saying that Mr. Merkin needed to hire some new people. The man and woman he'd had working there for years were leaving, and they were trying to find another husband and wife to take their place. But it was hard to find anyone willing to go along with the isolation."

She slowed the car and gestured out the window. "We're

getting close now. In just a few minutes you'll be able to see Magic Lake and Merkin Island for yourselves."

My seat belt jerked as I leaned forward to stare at the huge pine trees. I'd been so caught up in Aunt Doris's story that I hadn't noticed how wild the scenery was now. All signs of civilization had passed. There weren't any billboards or gas stations. We turned off the main highway and moved down a gravel road. Long miles of thick trees, overgrown shrubs, and tangled vines stretched in front of us. Then, far off to the right, I saw blue water.

Clarice rolled down her window. "Smell the pine trees?" she called. "And look! The water in that lake isn't blue! It's kind of turquoise-colored."

"That's why it's called Magic Lake," Aunt Doris said. "The color changes from one shade of blue to another as the sun moves above the water."

I was hanging out the window then, too. Aunt Doris turned right, down a narrow dirt road, and we were on a bluff high above the lake. Now I could see cottages set back in the trees. The water shimmered in the heat of noon, and there was a damp smell mingling in with the scent of the pines.

"Look at that black part right in the middle there," Clarice said, pointing toward the lake. "First there's the turquoise water and then there's a strip of black, and then there's the island. Is there a big drop-off there? Deep water always looks black."

Aunt Doris nodded. "That's another reason for the name of the lake. People say it's magic because there's no bottom in certain areas. Evidently this area was formed by huge glaciers in the last ice age. They gouged out the land to form the deep depression here. When they pushed the earth, they

formed an island in the middle of the lake, and a huge drop-off area between the shore and the island."

"A drop-off!" I shivered just thinking about how awful it would be to go running into the water and suddenly plunge in over my head. I'm scared to death of deep water. It's a joke, I guess, because I've always lived by Lake Michigan, and I go to the beach a lot. But the fact is that I can't swim and don't even want to learn. Splashing around on firm ground is fun enough for me.

"You don't have to worry about stepping off the drop-off though, Flee Jay," Aunt Doris said, as if reading my mind. "It's far out from the shore. You can walk for nearly a block and not have water over your waist."

"That's good." I glanced at the luggage piled on the seat beside me. "And I've got my inner tube, so I can float all over near the shore."

Clarice snorted. "I don't know why you're such a chicken in the water, Flee Jay. Fat has buoyancy, you know. You shouldn't have any trouble floating."

"Hey!" I shouted. "Do you—"

"Well, I didn't mean just *you,*" she added quickly. "I mean that *anybody* can float. Everybody has some fat."

Aunt Doris brought the car to a stop. "Here we are, girls. Just in time to keep you from another one of your 'comparisons of ideas.' " Grinning, she turned to open the door. "Want to come meet Mrs. Quist? I have to get the key from her."

"Not me," Clarice said. "I have to get all my notebooks in order."

Since she was staying, I decided to go along with Aunt Doris. I climbed from the car, noticing that we were in a circle of small white cottages. A sign in front of the one nearest to us said RENTAL OFFICE.

The lady in the office was talking on the telephone when we came in. She was a big woman with frizzy gray hair and a round red face. Her hair was pushed back by pink sunglasses, which matched her dangling pink earrings and her pink plastic sandals. Pink seemed to be her color, because there were pink flowers in the ruffly cotton dress she wore, too.

"My stars, you made it!" she cried to Aunt Doris when she finally hung up the phone. It sounded as though she thought we'd come from Mars. "Why, I wasn't expecting you until late this afternoon. You must have had light traffic all the way. Was the trip an easy one? I have your key right here. It's one of the new cottages and I know you'll be tickled with it. Is this one of those sweet little nieces you told me about? So what's happened to you since last summer, Doris, and what grade are you in, dear?"

But neither one of us got to answer any of the questions, because Mrs. Quist didn't stop talking long enough to let us. She told us all about the new cottage she had reserved for us, with long descriptions of how she had had to keep those carpenters on their toes. She gave a weather report for the week before and the week to come.

When we finally got back out the door, her voice followed us. "Just drive over to the cottage nearest to the hill," she called after us. "I'll try to skip over later to see how you're doing."

My mind was boggled trying to imagine a woman of her age trying to skip anywhere at all.

"So now you know Mrs. Quist," Aunt Doris said, starting the car. "She's a bit talkative."

"And bees are a bit busy," I replied.

"Ha!" Clarice said, staring into the backseat. "Bees are more than a *bit* busy, Flee Jay. They're busy all the time! You ought to—''

Aunt Doris and I never heard the rest, because we were laughing. ''There's nobody in the whole world like you, Clarice,'' she said.

''Thank goodness,'' I mumbled, and then I was as busy as a bee carrying all our stuff into the cottage. By this time it was well past noon, so I worked fast. For one thing I wanted to get out of my hot, wrinkled clothes, but there was an even more important reason that kept me moving that stuff in in such a big hurry. The sooner all the boxes were carried inside, the sooner we could have lunch.

I mean, new cottages and magic lakes are terrific and all that, but nothing can ever take the place of a peanut-butter, brown sugar, and banana sandwich.

Terrible Tragedies

"Hey, Flee Jay! Guess what?"

I tried to ignore Clarice's voice. We'd been splashing around in the water for almost three hours, and I was lying back in my inner tube happily floating. The water felt cool and clean beneath me as I let my mind and my body drift. Earlier I had used my hands like oars, and I had paddled back and forth near the shore. But now I was letting my arms and legs dangle over the sides. My knees were getting sunburned, but I didn't care. Sometimes you have to suffer to become beautiful, and the plainer you are, the more you have to suffer. I'm a realist, so long ago I prepared myself for a life of pain.

But it's not easy to ignore Clarice. "Did you hear me, Flee Jay?" she called. Her voice vibrated nearer. She had probably calculated sound waves and water waves and had paddled to a crucial spot, the very place where it would be impossible for me not to hear her. "I said I've just figured out a perfect murder, Flee Jay. Nobody would ever know it was a murder at all."

I squinted in her direction. She was hanging on the inside of her inner tube, her chin resting on the rim, her arms wrapped over the side. She'd been in that same position almost the whole time, yet here she was, already tanned, even on her legs, which, as far as I could see, never came near the rays of the sun. Maybe Clarice is so bright her thoughts can make her tan. I know that her brain activity heats up her head and keeps her hair dry. Her long blonde hair flashed in the sunlight as her inner tube bobbed in the water.

Sighing, I wrinkled my nose. The pain reminded me that it was sunburned, too. By evening I would look like a round red tomato topped by kinky red fuzz. Obviously my no-burn tanning lotion wasn't working. Advertising slogans seem to lose their meaning when I use them. My striped green bathing suit was supposed to make me long and slender, but it looked like a withered vine on a ripe tomato plant now.

"You could have the victim be floating on an inner tube," Clarice said, splashing nearer to me. "Right here in Magic Lake, just like we are. Let's say this woman is afraid of deep water and she can't swim. The murderer knows that. And you know about the drop-off here? If the victim was floating over the drop-off, somebody on shore or on the dock could shoot an arrow at the inner tube. It would lose air and sink, and the arrow would fall out and sink, too. Then the victim would drown, and there wouldn't be any evidence of murder. It would look like a terrible accident."

Her voice grew louder with enthusiasm. "Wouldn't that be a good plot for a television show, Flee Jay? Or maybe the murderer could loosen the air nozzle on the tube so that it would lose air as soon as it floated out over the drop-off."

I had the nozzle on my inner tube right beside my hand. It was screwed on tight. "I don't think that plot would work," I said. "If somebody is really afraid of water and can't swim, then she isn't going to float out over a drop-off, is she?"

"Aren't you afraid of the one in this lake?" Clarice asked.

"Sure. And that just proves what I said. You notice that I don't get near it, don't you?"

Clarice was practically beside me. I felt her inner tube bump against mine. "But we're floating over it right now."

"What?" I shot up so fast that my tube nearly flew out from under me. A fist seemed to wham me in the stomach and my throat tightened. The shoreline was far away. The water under me was pitch black. I tried to fight down the panic bursting inside of me. The inner tube seemed frail and flimsy now, and the dark, deep drop-off lurked beneath me, a monster with an open mouth.

I started flailing out with my arms and legs, churning and turning, trying to force myself away from that drop-off. All I could think about was how it would feel to sink deeper and deeper into water that went down so far nobody knew where the bottom was.

It was a lifetime before my tube started jerking through the waves toward the shore. I pushed and pulled and urged myself toward the dock. I didn't breathe again until I saw familiar yellow sand below me. Then I jumped off my inner tube and whirled around to face Clarice.

"You dork! You know I can't swim! You tried to kill me just like the woman in that dumb story you just told! You know I can't swim and—"

"But you had just floated over the edge, Flee Jay," she shouted, bobbing up and down inside her tube. "I was going to tell you. I *did* tell you!"

"Sure, after I was nearly killed! What if I had let go of that inner tube? I would have sunk right down to who knows where—probably China. You know I can't swim!"

"Honest, Flee Jay, I wouldn't have let you drown. I have my lifesaving badge."

I didn't care what she had. Angrily I threw my inner tube on the wooden planks and then I hoisted myself up beside it.

"You were hardly even over the edge," Clarice called up to me. She was carefully inching her inner tube onto the dock beside mine. Clarice is so neat she never throws *anything*. When she's sick, she doesn't even throw up.

I grabbed my towel and stomped away. "I'm going up to the cottage," I said, marching to the path, full of determination and dignity. Actually I wanted my sandals, too, but I knew I'd have to search for them in my pile of clothes scattered all over beside Clarice's neatly laid out shoes, lace anklets, and purse. I was too mad to lower myself to that. Barefoot, I started up the hill.

"You ought to put some shoes on!" Clarice shouted behind me. "There's poison ivy all over that hill, you know."

I cringed. My toes curled. But I kept right on walking. When I make up my mind that I'm right about something, it takes more than a few leaves to make me hesitate. I kept telling myself that the green leaves cluttering the path were tiny maple trees and I plowed right through them.

As soon as I had walked three yards beyond the beach and was hidden by the huge bushes, my feet started itching, and my idea about maple trees vanished. I was sure I was tromping through hoards of poison ivy clusters. The bushes and trees were so thick it was hard to find any path winding up the steep hill, but I kept going because I didn't want Clarice to know that her words had bothered me.

Bush branches and tree limbs caught at the towel I carried, and invisible birds shrieked and scolded from the midst of leaves and shrubs. It was hot and sticky. Going down that hill sure had been a lot easier than climbing back up it. I stopped to catch my breath. Bugs were buzzing all around me, and the daring ones were darting in to nibble on the remains of some tanning lotion on my neck. I peered through the shrubs to see if Clarice was still watching me.

I was higher than I'd thought. My anger had propelled me along like rocket fuel, and I had hardly noticed how fast I was going. Clarice was a tiny speck of pink against all the shimmering shades of blue down below.

From this distance, I could plainly see the drop-off yawning in the center of the lake far behind her. It was strange how quickly the yellow sand gleaming from the shoreline disappeared into the blackness of the deep water covering it.

Just looking down at it made me shiver. I turned around and started climbing faster. Poison ivy and heat exhaustion were bad, but they weren't as bad as drowning. I'd had all I wanted of swimming for that day.

At last I reached the cottage patio. Aunt Doris had been planning to sunbathe in a lounge chair there, but I saw that her chair was empty now. As I stood panting beside the screen door, the sound of voices came floating through the air.

"Oh my yes, I do hope it works," a quavery voice was saying. "I've always loved antiques, and now that I'm retired, I hope I can make a little income from this shop."

"Of course it will work." I recognized the voice of Mrs. Quist. "All tourists love to poke around in antique shops, and your location—"

The screen door squeaked when I opened it, and the women turned to look at me. Mrs. Quist's round face beamed when she saw me.

"It's Fly Jay!" she said happily.

"Flee Jay," I told her.

She waved her hand. "Oh, I knew it was some sort of bug. Awful name for a pretty girl, but then I know it's just a nickname. You young folks come up with the strangest names a person can imagine. This is Mrs. Coles, dear. She's opening an antique shop down the road across from the general store. I was just telling her that it's sure to be a big success, what with all the tourists we have coming and going."

I nodded toward the other gray-haired woman. She was as skinny as Mrs. Quist was fat. Her hair was wound in a braided band around her face, and she wasn't wearing anything as frivolous as a flowered dress or pink earrings. She was dressed plainly in wire-rimmed glasses, a dark sleeveless blouse, and dark slacks.

"Won't it be hard to find merchandise?" Aunt Doris asked her. "I mean, there can't be too many antiques available in these small cottages."

"Too bad you can't get old Mr. Merkin to sell some of his things to you," Mrs. Quist boomed out. "He has some beautiful old antiques, my friend Violet tells me. She's been working on the island for almost a year now."

"So you did help find some new employees for over there," Aunt Doris said.

Mrs. Quist shrugged and waved her hands modestly. "Oh, I didn't have a whole lot to do with it. Just passed the word around nearby towns. But I did make it my business to talk to the Gallaghers when they first got here. I knew it would get plenty lonely on that island, and I wanted them to know I was here if they needed me. Violet's a sweet woman, and all that, but I'll tell you something." She lowered her voice. "She's as frail as her name. Yes, that's the truth. Her husband tells her what to do and she does it, so she hasn't been able to visit me very much although I call to check on her all the time. Women need spunk, that's what I think. They need spunk."

She took a deep breath. "Now what was I saying? Oh, yes, the Gallaghers have a son, too, but he's not quite right, if you know what I mean. He's close to thirty, I'd venture, but he's got the brain of a six-year-old. It's too bad, too bad, but he's a dear boy just the same. The Gallaghers are fine people, and they've been glad to have a home and jobs even though Mr. Merkin *is* such a strange one."

Mrs. Coles cleared her throat. "Strange?"

"My stars," Mrs. Quist declared. "Strange isn't the word for him!" She stared at Mrs. Coles, obviously forgetting that she had used that word herself. Shaking her head, her earrings clattering, she whispered, "But who can blame the poor man for being so peculiar? He's had such terrible tragedies, you know."

"What tragedies?" Mrs. Coles asked.

Mrs. Quist sat back, folding her arms across her large chest. "Well, I don't know exact facts, of course, because I didn't live here when all of this happened years and years ago. But others have told me. When I bought this land, I learned as much as I could, and I've picked up tidbits of information here and there." She glanced toward me. "It's important to know all you can know, my dear. I don't approve of gossip and I'm not a nosy person, but I believe we all have to make an effort to get facts straight."

I nodded and tried to look wise. My own sister could not have said it better.

"It seems that Ezra Merkin's wife had a terrible accident years and years ago. She was out over that drop-off in a small boat when a sudden storm came in. Before she could row ashore, the waves had capsized the boat. It washed ashore days later, but her body was never found. It was an awful thing, an awful thing. A terrible shock."

"Her body is still out there?" I cried, suddenly imagining a skeleton floating under the black water.

Mrs. Quist's face quivered. "My stars! Oh, I don't think so. Underwater currents probably carried the body off years ago."

"The poor man!" Aunt Doris said. "And that's when he started living like a hermit?"

"Not right then." Mrs. Quist lowered her voice. "There was another terrible tragedy shortly after that one. Mr. Merkin had a daughter—Caroline. People say he poured all his love and affection on his daughter after his wife died. Then one night the awful thing happened." She paused dramatically, and her earrings went swinging back and forth in the sudden silence.

"One night when Mr. Merkin was out of town on business, young Caroline was kidnapped! Yes, taken right from her very bed. Right from the very house across this very lake. The ladder the kidnappers used was left right by her window."

Aunt Doris gasped. "But wasn't anyone there with her?"

"Oh my, yes. There was *always* someone hovering over Caroline, she being so precious and all. But nobody ever heard a sound. Not a single peep. The kidnappers must have drugged the child while she was still sleeping."

I felt cold all over. "And the police never found her? They never found the kidnappers?"

"Not a trace," Mrs. Quist declared. "Mr. Merkin had detectives out for years, but nothing was ever discovered. The odd thing was that there never was a ransom note either. The police said that perhaps the drug the kidnappers had given Caroline had been too strong and killed her. Others wondered if maybe the whole thing had been planned by Mrs. Merkin herself. There was gossip that Ezra Merkin wasn't a pleasant man to live with. Some said that maybe his wife didn't die in that boating accident, maybe she wanted to disappear, and then she had the child taken so that the two of them could live off on their own somewhere. But I've never put any faith in tales like that myself. Wouldn't that child have tried to get back to see her own father once she grew up? My stars, that kidnapping was almost forty years ago! No, I say Caroline Merkin died back then as a child. I say she's dead. Dead as a doornail.''

''And so that's why Mr. Merkin lives like a hermit on that island,'' Aunt Doris said.

''That's what people say,'' Mrs. Quist declared. ''What a tragedy! After Caroline was declared legally dead, why people say that Mr. Merkin just couldn't stand to go out in public. Everywhere he went, he thought he saw her. He was sure she wasn't dead, since he kept seeing her.''

Mrs. Coles leaned forward. ''And how old was this child?''

''Nine or ten, from what I've heard,'' Mrs. Quist replied. ''I've seen her picture often enough. She—''

We all turned as the patio door creaked open again. Clarice, her white towel draped around her shoulders like a fluttery cape, came gliding into the room. Her long blonde hair was already dry, and it looked almost gold in the late-afternoon sunlight.

Mrs. Quist gasped. Suddenly she jumped up so fast her chair fell with a great crash behind her. Her rosy face went white with shock. ''Caroline!'' she cried. ''Caroline!''

An Ageless Ghost

The next few seconds are blurred in my mind because my brain froze in surprise. All I can remember is Mrs. Quist clutching at the table and teetering back and forth, all trembly. Her mouth was like a circle and after taking one big breath, she seemed to be standing there without breathing.

"What's the matter?" Clarice cried, dropping her long white towel. Her purse clunked to the floor. "What's wrong?"

Her voice broke the spell. Mrs. Quist breathed again. "Mercy me. Mercy me!" she said hoarsely. "What a start you gave me, child, what a start!"

Aunt Doris reached over and pulled up the fallen chair. "Sit down, Edith. You look like you've just seen a ghost."

Panting, Mrs. Quist collapsed into her chair. Her face was turning rosy again. She pulled out a handkerchief from down the front of her dress. Nervously laughing, she mopped at her forehead. "I thought I *did* see a ghost! Oh, I feel like such a fool. Such a ninny! What must you all think of me? But it's amazing! This child looks just like—like—"

"You called her 'Caroline,' " Mrs. Coles said, leaning closer. She peered over the tops of her wire glasses. "You mean that you thought it was that little Merkin girl we were just talking about? The kidnapped child?"

"But what a thing to imagine! It was just a foolish mistake." Mrs. Quist's face grew even redder. She waved her hand. Her earrings clattered. "Oh, what a ninny I've become in my old age! Forgive me, my dears. What with all our talk about that poor dead child, I lost my wits. This child couldn't be Caroline Merkin. Of course not! That child was ten years old more than forty years ago! She's dead now, dead as a doornail. But this is the peculiar part—" She lowered her voice. "She looks just like those pictures of little Caroline. She's the spitting image of the girl in those old pictures."

"What pictures?" Clarice asked.

Mrs. Quist blinked at her. She pulled her dress forward and dropped the handkerchief back inside, then took another deep breath. "It was the white towel, like a cape it was. That's what did it. And the long blonde hair. And the way the sun blinded me for a minute there. In the pictures, Caroline had a white towel wrapped around her shoulders, and she had the same beautiful hair. The eyes are alike, too. Why, these two girls could be twins." Still marveling, she stared at Clarice again. "Twins, I tell you, twins." Her voice grew softer. "Do you think—do you suppose—that maybe . . ."

"Oh, I don't think they could be related," Aunt Doris said quickly. "My sister is her mother. Our name is Lenski. We never even knew anybody named Merkin. And now my sister's name is Saylor. She married Ron Saylor. He's never mentioned a relative named Merkin either. This is their younger daughter, Clarice. Clarice, this is Mrs. Quist. She's the woman who owns the rental cottages here. And this is Mrs. Coles. She's going to open an antique shop just down the road."

Clarice looked from one face to another, obviously not sure of what to say. Usually she has plenty to say about every topic under the sun. And topics away from our sun too. But this scene seemed beyond her understanding, completely out of our universe. Lookalikes of dead girls from forty years in the past don't make sense, and Clarice likes everything to be neat, logical, and orderly. Frowning, she kept staring at us.

"How'd that girl die?" she finally asked.

Mrs. Quist stood up. "Oh my, let's not talk about it anymore. I'm still feeling all nittery. Besides, I'd best skip off home. Heaven only knows how many phone calls I've missed while I've been sitting here. Magic Lake is getting more and more popular, and I'm mighty glad of it, what with these new cottages I've had built. Oh the expense! You wouldn't believe the expense! But enough about business. I'm sorry I scared the wits out of all of you that way. I must be getting foolish in my old age."

Mrs. Coles laughed. "Why, Edith Quist, how you carry on! You're not as old as all *that!* I'm sixty-two myself, and I bet you're nowhere near that age. You're not as old as you pretend." She patted the braids wound around her head. "I feel younger now than ever. This antique shop is giving me new purpose in life. But I'll be off now, too. I've got to get everything in shape for my grand opening."

As soon as the screen door shut behind them, Aunt Doris turned to us. "So girls, did you have a good time swimming?"

"How'd that girl die?" Clarice demanded. "What's ev-erybody talking about?"

"It was the strangest thing, honey. You know that Merkin family I was telling you girls about this morning? They had a—"

I decided that my report of almost drowning looked pretty puny beside a kidnapped ten-year-old who had almost turned up forty years later after being legally declared as dead as a doornail. It's my fate in life to think I have astonishing, eventful news only to find out that somebody with even bigger news has arrived just ahead of me. Probably after years of study, one of my ancient relatives rushed up to tell Queen Isa-bella that the world might not be flat on the same day Columbus sailed in from America. I went plodding off to the bedroom.

"Get dressed so you can go to the store for me, will you Flee Jay?" Aunt Doris called after me. "It's just a mile or so down the lakeshore road, and I need eggs for our potato salad." She didn't wait for my answer, so I decided that, like Mom's, her questions are really just polite commands.

Twenty minutes later Clarice and I were on our way to the general store. She plodded along all pink and white and proper. Her pink shorts weren't even wrinkled—the lace on her collar was fresh and white. My own clothes were a mess. Back home she had told me how to pack my suitcase scientifically, but I had told her to stuff it, and then I'd stuffed my clothes in a gym bag just to prove that I didn't care.

We were walking along the dirt road surrounding the lake. The trees were so thick I could hardly see the small cottages that I knew were hidden behind the huge bushes. A few sea gulls swooped down in the distance, ready for their evening meal. The late afternoon sun made everything look hazy. Every few minutes cars or trucks would whiz past us. Most were pulling huge boats. Clarice glared at the dust they created, brushing it off her clothes and her purse even though none of it actually stuck to her. She looked cross and cranky.

After walking in silence five minutes or so, I nudged her. "You didn't *have* to come, you know."

"Aunt Doris said I could peel potatoes or go with you. You know I hate touching potatoes with their skins still on. Worms probably crawled over them."

I shrugged and walked faster. Clarice can't stand getting her hands or face dirty. When she eats, she goes through napkins the way other people go through potato chips.

She cleared her throat. "I wanted to write some notes about that kidnapped girl." She pushed at her purse. The sunlight made the rhinestones on the handle sparkle. "It was weird when Mrs. Quist thought I looked so much like that dead girl. I wonder if Caroline Merkin really did die."

"Of course she did. Mrs. Quist said she was as dead as a doornail. Whatever that means."

Clarice took a deep breath, and I realized—too late—that I was in for another one of her lectures. "A doornail was a big nail used in door knockers in the sixteenth century," she said, "when buildings had those great big wooden doors. They pounded those nails in hard so that they never would come out. They had to be hit square on the head. Shakespeare used that idea in *Hamlet* when he had one character say that another character was as dead as a doornail. It means that there isn't any doubt someone is really dead."

Clarice's amazing facts were bad, but something even worse was beginning to bother me. My ankles were itching like crazy. I tried to sneak a peek at the skin there. Was I really getting poison ivy, the way Clarice had warned me I might?

Old Eagle Eyes saw me looking. "See?" she said. "I told you." She pointed at my ankles. "Poison ivy."

"It is not!" I made a face. "I have acne of the ankles, that's all. Lots of teenagers get that."

Clarice threw her hands to her hips. "Hah! You're not a teenager yet anyway."

Just as I was thinking about a snappy answer, I heard the sound of running water. Off the road to our right, I saw a small creek trickling on down to Magic Lake. "I'm going to wash my ankles in that water," I told Clarice. "Wait up here, will you? Study the wildflowers here by the road."

She took a deep breath as I started off. "You've got poison ivy. Just like I told you. Nanny, nanny, boo boo!"

I declined to dignify her words with an answer, so I just kept walking under the big trees. I followed the shallow creek as it moved closer to the lake, where it was much cooler. Right near the water, I sat down by an old tree and pulled off my sandals. The water felt good on my acne. In the cool shadows, I looked around the small cove. There were weeds and bushes and dead tree branches. The huge tree nearest me had almost been washed away by the lake. Its tangled roots were all exposed. "Like a nest of snakes," I whispered aloud, tracing some of the gnarled lines with my fingers.

I looked out over the water. In the distance, I saw the island, and I wondered about Mr. Merkin. Everything there looked shimmery and unreal. I squinted, wondering whether Mr. Merkin still thought he saw his daughter flitting around like an ageless ghost. I wondered what he would do if he saw Clarice. Would he think Caroline had come back from the grave, a lost lookalike returning?

I was feeling so caught up in thinking of the past that I nearly jumped out of my skin when Clarice called me.

"Flee Jay! Are you coming or aren't you?" she shouted from back on the hill.

I tried to shake the thoughts from my mind as I shook the water from my feet. When I reached Clarice, she sniffed. "You're the one who was in such a rush to get to the store, Flee Jay. What in the world were you thinking about back there?"

"Nothing," I told her. And in a way it was true. The things I had been thinking about weren't in the world at all, that was for sure. Not in any ordinary world, anyway.

"You wouldn't understand," I told Clarice. And that was true, too. And as we walked on, I still felt that same strange sense of eeriness. I wondered what it might be like over there on Merkin Island.

More Questions

After walking less than ten minutes more, we rounded another bend in the road and saw the "business section" for Magic Lake. There wasn't a whole lot to see—just a gas station, a small grocery store, and a boat-rental place. Across from them was a long yellow cement building with a sign in front: COLES ANTIQUES—GRAND OPENING SOON.

Clarice turned toward the grocery store. "Hope I'll be able to buy a book or a magazine."

I glanced at a cardboard notice, advertising the daily special in the window: KRACKERS FOR KOZY KAMPERS. "Don't count on anything being very literary in here," I whispered as we went inside.

A bell rang when we opened the door. I stood a moment blinking. After the bright sunlight outside, the store seemed dark and gloomy. The only things I could see clearly were two white signs. One said that lottery tickets were available, and the other said that the name of the store owner was Michael Brock.

"Looks like the magazines are in the back," Clarice said, moving off.

A dark-haired man was reading a newspaper behind the cash register to my right. His face was so tanned it looked like leather, and he had deep lines etched into his forehead.

With his feet propped up on the counter, he looked so relaxed that I knew he had to be the owner, Mr. Brock himself. "Can I help you?" he asked, slowly easing himself to his feet.

I already had the carton of eggs and he was giving me my change when Clarice was back. "Guess I won't get a magazine after all," she said. "They were all about hunting or fishing."

The coins bounced on the counter and scattered to the floor. The man had jerked forward, his tall skinny body rigid as he stared at Clarice. His dark eyebrows froze into question marks over his eyes. Then almost as abruptly, he bent to get the money, and stammered an apology. "S-Sorry. But she looked like—"

"Like Caroline Merkin," I finished for him.

The lines in his forehead danced. "Someone else noticed that, too?"

Clarice moved closer. "The lady who owns the rental cottages said I looked like that girl who was kidnapped forty years ago. She said she had seen pictures."

"Oh." He slumped his scrawny shoulders and heaved a huge breath. "I thought I was seeing things for a minute there. Thought I was seeing a ghost. You do look a lot like Caroline Merkin. She was a playmate of mine when we were kids, but I didn't think anybody else around here would remember her. I wasn't thinking about pictures." He nodded. "Sure, there would be plenty of pictures." He looked at Clarice even more closely. "Your hair is the same—your size is the same. Maybe you're a relative."

I shook my head. "We never knew anybody named Merkin."

He kept staring. "Maybe Caroline's mother married again. She could have had another child with a different name."

"We thought Caroline's mother died in a boating accident," Clarice told him.

Mr. Brock shrugged. "Well, that was the official story, all right. But those of us who lived here wondered about that. I was only a youngster at the time, but I remember the gossip. Oh, there was plenty of guessing and gossip."

Clarice pushed at her big purse. I could see that her fingers were itching to get at a pen so she could start writing in one of her notebooks. "What was the gossip?" she asked. She looked so eager to listen that Mr. Brock obviously felt he had to talk.

He leaned against his cash register. "Well, it was a long time ago, so it shouldn't matter what I tell you now. The story was that Ezra Merkin and his wife fought constantly, and I knew it was true because Caroline told me. She was scared to death of her father. Told me so lots of times when we'd go fishing or swimming. Anyway, Mrs. Merkin wanted to take her daughter and run off, but he controlled the money, and he wouldn't let her leave. When that boat was found upturned in the water after the storm, there were plenty of people who said that Mrs. Merkin had staged her own death so that she could get away."

His voice faded away, and the drone of a fly was the only sound. I cleared my throat. "Mrs. Quist said they never found her body."

"And they never will—not in this lake, anyway. That's my theory. Oh, but I remember how they tried! Day after day they searched that drop-off area, but nothing surfaced. They even shot off dynamite, hoping that the vibrations would bring the body up, but that didn't help. The lake's got no bottom in some places, you know. If something was sucked down into the caverns below, it would never show up again." He stood up straighter. "No matter. Lots of us have always felt that Mrs. Merkin was never in that lake in the first place."

Clarice leaned on the counter. "And when Caroline was kidnapped, you think—"

"Why, the mother arranged it herself. That's what we thought." He sighed. "No way of knowing now, though. It's ancient history. Most of the folks who knew Mrs. Merkin and Caroline have died or left the area long ago. Old Ezra Merkin never leaves that island. It's all in the past, all in the past. It just came back to me when I saw you, that's all." He stared at Clarice again. "You're a dead ringer for little Caroline Merkin."

"A dead ringer for someone as dead as a doornail," I mumbled, but he didn't hear me.

"But say!" As he waved away the fly buzzing around his head, he seemed to be trying to wave away the past, too. "I didn't mean to go rambling on like this. You kids don't want to hear about old gossip. I just—"

The bell clanged again, and a large man walked in. "Got any lucky lottery tickets today?" he asked. "I sure could use a hundred thousand dollars!"

"Gosh," I whispered to Clarice as we left the store. "Did you hear that? The instant lottery tickets are paying a hundred thousand dollars this month! Want to go cash in our eggs and get a couple tickets?"

Clarice snorted. "The chances of winning the big prize in a lottery are more than a million to one! You'd be throwing away Aunt Doris's money. Besides, you have to be eighteen in order to buy those tickets. Keep the eggs, Flee Jay. Keep the eggs."

"Oh." I grinned. "Guess the yolks on me."

Clarice gave me such a glare that I knew she didn't get the humor, but she was too proud to ask. Joking with Clarice is like roller-skating on ice. You can do it, but you're not going to get very far. We marched toward the road. "I'm hungry," I said. "Let's try to—"

"Shhhh—someone's calling us." She gestured to the cement building across the street. Mrs. Coles was standing in the doorway, beckoning to us. "Girls—could you come over here for a moment?

"Come in, come in," she whispered when we reached her store. She pulled us inside and shut the door. The smell of mothballs and old attics settled around me. There was a small fan blowing, but the room was hot and stuffy.

It was crowded, too. Huge dark cabinets towered from the walls, and long tables were loaded with oil lamps and ugly vases. There were round wooden tables with feet like animal claws and chairs with curved legs and velvet seats. A huge grandfather clock stood just to the right of the screen door.

"The strangest thing has happened," Mrs. Coles told us. "I wasn't sure how to handle this, but then I thought it wouldn't harm anyone if I talked to you two girls. After all, you're even newer around here than I am."

"Couldn't you talk to Mrs. Quist?" I asked, and Clarice kicked me, right on the acne on my ankle. I knew she was warning me to keep quiet and let Mrs. Coles say anything she wanted to say. She's always telling me that if I don't keep my mouth shut, I'll never be a good detective. I wanted to kick her back, but Mrs. Coles was looking at me.

"Well, that's just it," she said, "It's *about* Edith Quist. And that's why I'm so confused. How well do you girls know her?"

"I only met her yesterday," I told her. "And you saw what happened this afternoon. Clarice only met her today."

"Well, I don't know what to say." Mrs. Coles rubbed at her face, and I saw that it was smudged with dirt. Her hands were dusty and dirty, and she waved them as she talked.

Long pieces of her hair straggled out from her braid. "I don't know Edith well at all. Only met her a few weeks ago when I rented this building. She seemed nice enough, and we've talked a few times. But why would she trick us the way she did today? I simply can't understand it. Sit down, girls, sit down. Let me show you something here."

I plopped down in a horsehair chair near the grandfather clock and then I was immediately sorry. It pricked the back of my legs. My sunburn suddenly began itching. Clarice just stood beside me. That fabulous brain of hers must have warned her about prickly antique fabric. No wonder people sitting in those chairs in old-fashioned pictures have such sour expressions on their faces. They must have wanted to scratch themselves in personal places.

Mrs. Coles pulled a metal box off a table. She pointed at the dusty shelf beside her grandfather clock. Only a small pathway forward was clear. "After I left your cottage this afternoon and came back here, I found this box on that shelf. It must have been left by the previous shop owner. I was just sorting things when I came upon these two pictures. They're practically antiques—must have been taken forty years ago anyway. Just take a look." She handed each of us a picture.

I glanced down to see a fat seven- or eight-year-old girl. She was staring at the camera as though she thought it might bite her. Her dark hair was short and curly, and she was frowning as she waved at the camera with her left hand. She looked the same in Clarice's picture, but she was holding a big teddy bear in her right hand.

"Looks like the clothes they wore in the 1940s," Clarice said. "Is she a friend of yours?"

Mrs. Coles peered at us over the tops of her wire glasses. "But don't you know who this is?"

"How would we know?" I asked.

"Oh my, I didn't tell you! Look on the back, that's what

made my head spin when I happened to turn one of those pictures over. And then I found it on both of them. That's what confused me about Edith's story. Just look on the back."

I flipped over the photo I held, and then caught my breath. It was a good thing I was sitting, with my bag of eggs on my lap. We might have had an antique omelet on the floor. "Caroline Merkin," I cried. "It says here that this is Caroline Merkin!"

"Yes." Mrs. Coles reached for her pictures. "So you can see why I was confused. Why would Edith Quist say that Caroline Merkin was blonde and slender, like Clarice? She doesn't look like Clarice at all!"

"But the man at the store said that—" I wasn't able to finish my sentence because Clarice kicked my ankle again.

"Maybe somebody showed her pictures of a child they *thought* was Caroline Merkin," Clarice said. "Maybe someone made a mistake, and Mrs. Quist didn't know it. Couldn't that be what happened?"

There was a slight movement at the screen door, but when we all looked, the doorway was empty. Mrs. Coles frowned. "Well, I suppose that might explain it all right. But Edith seemed so sure! When I accidentally came upon these pictures, with the name clearly written on the back, why, I just didn't know what to think. Do you think I ought to show them to Edith?"

I wasn't used to having adults ask me what to do, but Clarice just blinked and smiled. "You could show them to other people too," she said. "Maybe someone else will know who made a mistake."

"That was weird, wasn't it," I said as we left the store. "Do you really think Mrs. Quist made a mistake? I mean Mr. Brock said you looked just like that kidnapped girl, too, and he really knew her."

"Mrs. Quist said she saw pictures, too," Clarice told me, "but it couldn't have been those. Yeah, Flee Jay, it's weird all right."

"I wonder who wrote Caroline Merkin's name on the back of those pictures," I said. "Do you suppose the owner of Mrs. Coles's building wrote it years and years ago?"

Clarice shook her head. "No. Nobody did that, Flee Jay. The pictures were taken more than forty years ago, okay, but the name was written with a ballpoint pen. I could tell by the ink. There weren't any ballpoint pens then. Not with that special felt tip, anyway."

The sunburn on my shoulders began to throb, and the poison ivy on my ankles was burning, but the questions in my mind bothered me the most. "But why would anybody try to pretend that girl was Caroline Merkin by writing her name on a picture of a stranger?" I hugged my bag closer as another big question raced through my mind. "Who would have a reason to write the wrong name on old pictures?"

"*If* it's the wrong name," Clarice said.

"Well of course it's the wrong name!" I blurted. "Both Mrs. Quist and Mr. Brock said you look just like Caroline Merkin. You don't look one bit like that girl in Mrs. Coles's pictures."

For once I was so right that Clarice couldn't think of an argument. She shifted her purse to her other arm, and we hurried along the hot, dusty road in silence.

Worthless Clues

After walking along for more than ten minutes, I was hot, uncomfortable, and hungry. I gave up thinking about the old pictures and started thinking about food. As we passed the small creek, I nudged Clarice. "I think these eggs must be hard-boiled by now. Want to go sit by the water and eat them?"

"Nope. I'm thinking."

I don't know which is worse—Clarice talking when I want her to be quiet or Clarice being quiet when I want her to talk. She was marching along with her head held up high. That's her "listening" position. She says she pretends her ears are antennae and she can hear more that way, but it sounds weird to me. Ears are ears.

I noticed that she seemed to be looking over in the woods near the lake, but there was nothing special there that I could see. Thick weeds and dead shrubs were clumped in piles along the side of the road. Sprawling pine trees blocked the view of the water.

"Somebody's been following us," Clarice suddenly whispered. "I'm going to find out who it is. Just act natural."

"What?" I was so surprised I couldn't even think what acting natural meant. My body went stiff, and my head didn't seem to fit on my neck anymore. I took a quick look behind us. The road was absolutely empty. I breathed a sigh of relief. "You're loony, Clarice. Nobody's there."

"Someone has been following us for the last ten minutes, Flee Jay. In the trees and bushes over there. Can't you hear? Every time we go faster, he goes faster, too."

I tried to block out the sound of the crunching gravel under our feet. There was a faint swishing sound in the shrubs on our left. As I cautiously looked in that direction, I saw a flash of white deep between the trees. Clarice was right. Someone was quietly pushing branches aside to watch us, moving just as steadily as we moved. A branch cracked under invisible footsteps. Chills raced across the back of my sunburned neck. "Maybe we'd better start running."

Clarice shook her head. As a car drew nearer, she stared right at the spot where the bushes were swaying. "How come you're following us?" she shouted. "Come on out here!" She leaned closer to me. "See that car coming? If we need help, we can get it."

But as soon as the figure stepped out into the clearing beside the road, I saw that we wouldn't need help. This man was as big and maybe as old as Aunt Doris, but he was grown-up only in his body. Mom and I work in the Special Olympics every year, and this man was exactly like some of the people there. Smiling, he blinked at us from under the brim of his "Tigers" hat. As he twisted the ends of his Mickey Mouse shirt, he stared at Clarice. "Hi. I'm Ronnie. Who're you?"

At that same instant, the car coming toward us pulled over and stopped. Mrs. Quist stuck her head out the window. "Why, hello there, girls," she called, turning off the motor. As she climbed out, red earrings dangled. The frames on her sunglasses were red too. I saw that she had changed her flowered dress to bright red slacks and a striped shirt. I know

that stripes are supposed to make you look thinner, and maybe that's why she had bought the shirt, but it wasn't working. Mentally I tossed out all the striped shirts in my wardrobe. Her lipstick was bright red, too, slightly smeared on one side. She beamed at us. "I see you've met Ronnie Gallagher."

"Well, not really," I told her. "He was following us."

Mrs. Quist clacked her tongue. "Oh, Ronnie thinks he's an Indian sometimes," she said. "He rows the boat over from the island and hides in the bushes along the shore. He didn't mean to scare you girls. Ronnie wouldn't hurt a soul."

"Indian," Ronnie echoed, smiling and pointing to himself. "Indian."

"Did you come to get something from Mr. Brock's store?" she asked him, talking slower and even louder, the way some people do when they're talking to people who don't understand English.

He pulled a paper from his pocket. "Milk. Bread. And—and—"

"His mother always writes things down just in case Ronnie forgets," Mrs. Quist told us as she looked at the note. "She just has to hope that he understands and brings home what she asks for." She lowered her voice to a loud whisper. "He can't read, you know, poor thing, but whoever's in the store helps him a bit. But we can't watch him all the time. And every now and then he makes a mistake. Why, just last week Violet told me he came home with a loaf of bread just stuck in the packing bag. He'd taken the plastic wrapper off, and the slices were scooting around loose. Can you imagine such a thing? Ronnie couldn't explain why he'd done that. Now why in the world would he want to do a thing like that?" She didn't wait for our answer. "Did you ever find that bread wrapper?" she asked Ronnie, but he only grinned.

She threw up her hands. "Well, enough chitchat, girls. I

saw you walking and thought I'd give you a lift. I've got to get a few things from the store. Want a ride there, Ronnie?" As he jumped into the front seat, she turned back to us. "You want to drive down and back with me? Ronnie will take his boat home. He usually leaves it right down by the store's boat dock. Isn't that a fine way to travel, though? All cool and nice on the water. You two look hot and tired. You've had a busy day. What've you been up to? And do you want that lift?"

Clarice looked toward the car. Ronnie had moved over behind the steering wheel, and he was pretending to drive. "So he's the one you told us about. He lives on that island with Mr. Merkin?"

Mrs. Quist nodded. "It's not a bad life for him, I guess. Ronnie loves boating and fishing. Last winter he spent hours out on the ice in his fish shanty. Can you think why anybody would want to freeze that way? It beats me, girls, it beats me. And what if the ice melts? It gives me the heebie-jeebies just thinking about it, that's what. Anyway, island life is fine for him. It's his mother I worry about. Poor Violet hardly ever gets to see people. Her husband isn't very sociable, so it doesn't much matter to him, but she'd like to talk to somebody now and again. Don't you think anybody would? You know, girls, I had a little idea this afternoon, but I haven't checked with Violet. Do you think that—"

The car horn blasted. Ronnie smiled and waved out the window.

Mrs. Quist waved back. "He must have taken quite a shine to you. Ronnie's afraid of most strangers. Do you suppose people have been mean to him in the past? Why, who could do a thing to hurt him? He's as gentle as a kitten. But there's no accounting for what some folks might do, no accounting at all. Isn't that right? But he likes you two. It's plain to see that."

"Maybe he's seen pictures of Caroline Merkin like you did, and he thought Clarice was Caroline, too," I said. "Maybe that's why he followed us."

"What?" A flicker of surprise raced across Mrs. Quist's rosy face. Then she shook her head. "Oh, I doubt that, girls. He wouldn't remember a face in a photograph. Besides, Violet tells me Mr. Merkin doesn't have pictures of his family anywhere in the house. Isn't that a strange thing?" As the car horn blared again, she turned. "Well, I got to be going. Want that lift? I dasn't stand here chatting with you anymore. I've got to get back home before my show starts. Do you like television much?"

I was ready to jump inside the car, but Clarice shook her head. "We're almost to the cottage. But thanks anyway, Mrs. Quist."

"How come you did that?" I asked as soon as the car had driven off. "I'm tired of walking."

"I need to have some peace and quiet for thinking, Flee Jay. If we'd gone with Mrs. Quist, we'd have been stuck at that store another half hour. She always pretends that other people keep her talking, but she's the one. Words just sort of pour right out of her."

"But we could have told her about those pictures Mrs. Coles has. We could have asked her some questions. Mrs. Quist seems to like asking questions herself, so it would have been easy."

Clarice frowned. "But Mrs. Quist never gives time for anybody to answer her questions. No, I don't think questions to Mrs. Quist would help get us many answers right now. We need to get the facts in order before we ask anything. I can find out more from my own notebooks once I write down the facts we learned this afternoon."

"Facts? What facts? My gosh, Clarice, I've been with you

the whole time, and we haven't found out anything at all. We've only come up with a whole bunch of questions."

"You haven't been listening. You haven't been thinking. We've learned lots of facts. Facts that could be important clues."

"Name one."

"Mrs. Quist is left-handed."

"So why's that important?"

"I don't know. But it's a fact, and I need to write down all the facts I can get, even if they don't seem to matter much. Detectives never know what will help them solve a mystery. Something strange is going on here at Magic Lake. How can I look exactly like a girl who has been dead as a doornail for forty years? How come Mrs. Coles found that girl's name on the back of some old pictures that don't look anything at all like me? How come the pictures are so old but the name on the back is so recent?"

I didn't have any answers, but I had a question about what she had just said. It's always risky asking Clarice anything, because she usually gives a whole lecture when she answers one single question. But sometimes my thirst for knowledge makes me willing to risk a flood. "I didn't see Mrs. Quist write anything. How do you know she's left-handed?"

"Her lipstick was darker on the right side. Women who are right-handed put a stronger pressure on the left side of their mouths with their lipsticks, and women who are left-handed put pressure on their right."

In my mind I traced the way I put on my own lipstick when I use it. I always started on the left side, and I'm right-handed. "I wish I was smart instead of beautiful," I mumbled, but Clarice ignored me.

"And Mrs. Coles is left-handed, too," she went on.

"But Mrs. Coles wasn't wearing any lipstick!"

"She had ink smeared on the fingers of her left hand."

"I never noticed that."

"Face it, Flee Jay," Clarice said, pushing her purse higher on her arm. "You never notice anything. Bet you don't know the brand name of our television set, and yet for two or three hours every day you look at the screen with the word written right there."

I jerked to a halt, all prepared to tell her that she was crazy. But then I realized it. I truly didn't know what brand name was there by the screen. There was a word there, I knew for sure, but for the life of me I couldn't think what it was. I'll bet no normal kid ever notices television brand names. "I don't like to clutter my brain with useless information," I said stiffly.

She ran ahead, her ugly purse dangling. Now her genius side was gone, and her bratty side was back. "Nanny, nanny, boo, boo!" she called back. "You can't do what I do!"

As I've said before—life with Clarice is difficult.

But her words did give me a great idea. If Mrs. Coles had ink smeared on her hand, could it have been there because she wrote Caroline Merkin's name on those pictures herself? I couldn't imagine why she'd do that. Then I wondered if Clarice was wondering about the same things.

I marched along wishing I had looked at the color of the ink more closely. I had a feeling that this clue wasn't worthless at all. But I didn't know what to do with it.

Vandals and Lies

As we hurried to the cottage, thunder boomed in the west. We raced in the door just as the sky opened up and the rain poured down.

At first I thought that the weather would ruin at least one night of our vacation, but it didn't turn out that way at all. Aunt Doris, Clarice, and I had fun anyway. When the electricity went off around ten o'clock, we lighted candles and laughed about how strange the shadows looked as they danced around the walls. We sang songs and roasted marshmallows in the fireplace. By bedtime I was feeling real sisterly affection for Clarice. But then she had to go and spoil it all just as I was putting some lotion on my face.

"Don't forget to put the skin cream on that acne on your ankles," she told me, giggling.

"Be careful," I warned her. "You may end up being as dead as a doornail if you don't stop teasing me."

"Maybeeeee I ammmm allllllreadddddy," she wavered, trying to sound like a ghost.

Later, lying in bed listening to the wind billow the waves out in the lake, I thought about all of the weird things that had happened that day. My thoughts swirled inside my head just like driftwood swirling out in Magic Lake, and the possibilities seemed as endless as the water out over the drop-off. I kept remembering the shock on the faces of both Mrs. Quist and Mr. Brock when they saw Clarice. Then I remembered the fat, dark girl in the old photographs and the name on the back. As I drifted off to sleep, I decided that Magic Lake had given us all the mysteries we could handle. Surely the next day would be peaceful and quiet.

But the next morning I found I had guessed wrong. We were just finishing breakfast when Mrs. Quist came hurrying up to the cottage. "You'll never guess what happened!" she called through the screen door.

She kept talking as Aunt Doris let her in. She was wearing a pink housecoat and slippers with big fuzzy pink balls on them. I knew she must have been really excited because she had left her house without putting on any makeup or dangling earrings.

She took a deep breath. "Marie Coles just called me. Her store was vandalized! Can you believe such a thing happening here at Magic Lake? Marie walked into her shop this morning and found her store in a terrible mess. Why, she was so surprised she rushed right back to her cottage and called me. Somebody had broken in there during the night! Furniture was upside down, vases were broken, books were tossed, and newspapers were ripped to pieces." She paused to take a deep breath, and her double chin trembled. "It's shocking, that's what I call it—shocking! Things like that don't happen here, that's all, they just don't happen here. We're all decent people around here and—"

"Was anything stolen?" Clarice asked.

Mrs. Quist reached into her pocket and pulled out a tissue. "Mercy," she said, mopping her face. "I must look like a scarecrow. I ran right over without even dressing. I'm usually up at dawn and dressed right away, but today I've been a bit of a slowpoke. I've been working on my bank statement.

Oh my, what a lot of work that is! No, no, nothing was stolen, thank goodness, but Marie called me because she wondered if you two girls had seen anyone suspicious on the way home last night."

"The only people we saw were you and Ronnie," I told her.

"Maybe this Ronnie had something to do with it," Aunt Doris suggested.

Mrs. Quist shook her head so hard that her gray curls danced. "Oh my no! Ronnie Gallagher would never do a thing like that. You could stake your life on that! No, whoever did this to Marie Coles's shop has to be vicious."

"Could it be that someone is trying to frighten her away?" Aunt Doris asked. "Was anybody upset because she was opening a new business here?"

"No, no, nothing like that. Why, we were all pleased as punch when we heard another business was setting up here. Why, all of us in business were tickled when she rented that vacant building. The more there is to do and see here at Magic Lake, the more people will visit, and the better off we'll all be. Property values will go up and—"

"Did Mrs. Coles talk to Mr. Brock?" Clarice asked. "His store is right across the street. Was it vandalized, too?"

"Yes, she talked to him right away. He thought someone had tampered with his locks, but nobody broke in. He has double bolts on all his doors, you know. Marie's locks were just too meager, that's all there is to it. But who would imagine that you needed strong locks in a quiet place like here? Oh, it's disgraceful, that's what, disgraceful. It takes a special kind of person to vandalize a place, and I know just who would do it." Mrs. Quist folded her arms. "Oh yes, I know just who."

"Who?" Clarice cried. "Who?"

"Hooligans, that's who."

All three of us stood staring, but Mrs. Quist had stated her opinion, and that was as far as she was going to go, even if it meant nothing at all.

Aunt Doris finally ventured a question. "But do you know who these hooligans might be?"

"Mercy no! How would *I* know any hooligans?"

She had stumped us with that question, so we stood there quiet as she turned toward the door. "But I'd best skip on home now and get dressed. I have an appointment at the bank this morning about my loan. What a lot of bother! What a lot of bother! I can't even get down there to help Marie clean up.

"Did Mrs. Coles call the police?" Clarice asked.

Mrs. Quist paused with her hand still on the door. "No, she didn't. I asked the same thing, but she said she didn't want the police involved in this. She thought it would be bad publicity for her store. She wouldn't want customers to think they were buying damaged merchandise. Nothing was stolen, you know. It's just a matter of cleaning everything up again."

"It's a shame," Aunt Doris said. "A real shame."

But Mrs. Quist didn't seem to hear her. She was staring at Clarice again. "I couldn't help thinking of you last night. You're so much like that lost child. A real lookalike." She hesitated another few moments and then opened the door. "But say! Don't keep me talking here any longer. I've got to get home and get dressed." She hurried out and the screen door banged behind her.

Aunt Doris looked out after her. "No more rain, thank goodness. But it's too dark and gloomy for swimming or sunning this morning. I think I'll do some reading. How about you?"

Clarice looked up from her notebooks. "Let's go help Mrs. Coles clean up her store, Flee Jay. Want to?"

My mouth dropped open in surprise, but Aunt Doris smiled. "What a nice idea! She'll be glad to have some help, I'll bet. You were sweet to think of helping her, Clarice."

I knew that sweetness had nothing to do with it. Just like me, Clarice wanted to get in on another mystery. I made up my mind to notice everything once we got to the shop. I would even try Clarice's trick about imagining special antennae on my head. Clarice could write her facts in her notebook, and I would keep the facts in my head. We'd see which one of us could come up with some answers first.

When we walked into Mrs. Coles's store, her big grandfather clock was chiming eleven, and she was busily picking up newspapers. The place was still messy, but it didn't look nearly as bad as I had thought it would.

"What a nice thing to do!" she said when Clarice told her that we'd come to help. Pushing back her straggling hair, she gestured around the room. "But oh, my, I feel so foolish carrying on the way I did when I called Edith to report what I found this morning. Things aren't nearly as bad as I first thought. It was the shock, you see. That's what made me call Edith that way. But I'm afraid I overestimated the damage."

Clarice was looking at the door. "Somebody must have kicked this in. The lock is broken off the side."

Mrs. Coles nodded. She poked her glasses back farther up on her nose. "The door was hanging open when I got here. I have a burglar alarm, but I guess it didn't work."

"So it happened between ten and two," Clarice said. "That's when the electricity was off last night."

I hadn't known that. When Clarice had fixed the clock early that morning, I hadn't thought it made any difference about how many hours we had lost. Good grief, detectives are supposed to notice absolutely everything, I guess. I waved my imaginary antennae and looked and listened.

"I'm grateful that nothing was stolen," Mrs. Coles was saying. "And the vases that were broken were some of my cheaper ones. Thank goodness they didn't get into the good china in the china cabinets. The vandals didn't do as much damage as they could have. They could have stolen some valuable pieces, but they must not have known much about antiques. That's why I told Edith it probably was teenagers."

She kept talking about how grateful she was that nothing serious had happened as we all three picked up old books and righted old chairs.

Half an hour later, the store looked fairly neat again. "You've been a big help, girls," Mrs. Coles told us. "Could I get you a treat at Mr. Brock's store? I'd be glad to give you a little something for your work."

An ice-cream cone sounded good to me—one with a double dip. But before I could say anything, Clarice shook her head. "No, no, nothing like that, thanks. But I wonder if we could see something."

Mrs. Coles nodded. "Of course, of course. The old doll? Is that what you want to see?"

"Those old pictures you showed us yesterday," Clarice answered. "I wondered if I could look at them again."

Mrs. Coles's face creased into puzzled frowns. "Well, certainly, certainly." She reached up for the metal box on the top shelf near her grandfather clock. As she dragged the box forward, she caught her breath. "This is strange! It feels so light that one would think—" She pulled it down and then looked at us, blinking over the tops of her glasses. Her quavery voice sounded even more shaky. "But this box is empty now! It's empty!"

I jerked forward. "The vandals *did* steal something then? They stole the pictures you showed us yesterday? But—"

Mrs. Coles quickly shoved the empty box up on the shelf

again. "Oh my. Maybe I moved those things myself, girls! I might have done and just plain forgot because of all the excitement of the break-in. Yes, that's it. That must be it." She looked at Clarice. "I'll find everything later, and let you see those old pictures then. I'm sorry I was so forgetful, children. It must be old age."

She kept apologizing as we backed out the door. The minute we were outside, I turned to Clarice. "Do you think she really put those pictures somewhere else and forgot?"

"Nope." Clarice grinned at me as she hopped down the steps. "You're getting smarter, Flee Jay."

"It didn't take a genius to figure that one out," I said. "She looked so confused and guilty when you asked to see those pictures that I knew something was screwy. But why would she lie about moving them?"

Clarice grinned at me. "Now you're sounding like a real detective, Flee Jay."

I hate to admit it, but praise from Clarice is so rare that I felt like a peacock spreading its feathers.

"And here's another important question," she said, nudging me. "Why would anybody want those old pictures?"

My feathers fell. I didn't have the slightest idea of the answer to that—in fact, I hadn't even thought of the question.

"It's getting hot," I said. "Maybe splashing around in the water will cool our brains. Beat you back to the cottage!"

Clarice won, but I didn't care. There are more important things in life than winning. And eating is one of them. We had a great lunch.

An Exciting Plan

By late afternoon the sun was so bright again that we all were down at the lake. I forced all thoughts of vandals and old pictures out of my mind. Maybe I couldn't come up with any answers on this vacation, I told myself, but I still had a chance to get tanned and gorgeous.

Well—at least I could get tanned.

So I was lying on a beach towel on the dock, and Aunt Doris was sitting in one of the lounge chairs beside me. Clarice was paddling in her inner tube far out in the water, but I still didn't want any part of trying that myself. The sea gulls were quiet, and the water made little lapping sounds, almost lulling me to sleep. The dock was warm, and I soon felt drowsy, but I struggled to stay awake. After all, you have to turn over now and then to get an even tan.

If I squinted my eyes and peered to the east, I could see the hazy outlines of the island. Every time I glanced that way, I wondered what it might be like to live there. Images of vandals, hermits, a disappearing woman, and a kidnapped child whirled around in my brain along with pictures of myself all bronzed and beautiful. And I guess all of them were equally impossible. I was almost asleep when suddenly Aunt Doris bolted forward.

"Edith! Did you decide to join us for a swim?"

Mrs. Quist was tromping toward the dock, panting and looking almost as warm and bright as the sun. She was wearing an orange flowered dress, and she was mopping at her forehead with a big white handkerchief.

"Swim!" she cried as she reached us. "My goodness, what an idea! Why, if I jumped in the water, the waves would wash up and flood the whole beach. Wouldn't they? Why, I'd have to buy my bathing suit in a tent shop!" Mopping her face, she laughed. "No, I'm not here to swim. I'm here to talk a few minutes. Soon as I catch my breath, I mean. Mercy, that hill leading down here gets steeper every year! I won't be walking back up it, you can bet on that. I'll walk along the shore and move up gradual-like."

She dragged another lounge chair forward and plopped down into it. "I have a little plan to ask you about, but I'm worried about Marie. She wasn't at her shop when I came back from town. And I can't call her there now because her phone isn't connected there yet. I wonder how she's doing."

"Apparently she's doing all right," Aunt Doris said. "The girls went down to help her this morning, and they got the whole place back in order. Things weren't nearly as bad as she had first thought, I guess."

"That's good." Clacking her tongue, Mrs. Quist leaned back in her chair. "What a way to start a new business! It's a miracle that nothing was stolen."

"Mrs. Coles had some pictures," I blurted. "She thought they were pictures of Caroline Merkin, but she couldn't find them."

"Maybe the vandals took them," Clarice said suddenly. She had paddled up beside the dock, and she was staring at us.

"My stars!" Mrs. Quist cried. "Pictures of Caroline Merkin?"

"Maybe they were the same ones you saw," Clarice told her.

"Why, they might be," Mrs. Quist said slowly. "They just might be. But it seems strange anybody would take them. Maybe Marie just tucked them away somewhere and forgot she did it. I do that all the time myself. Why, if my head wasn't stuck right on my body, I'd go off and forget it, sure as God made little green apples." She burst out with a booming laugh then, startling a dozing sea gull right off the end of the dock.

I was just about to tell her what the girls in Mrs. Coles's pictures looked like, but she leaned forward and kept talking.

"But say! I wanted to tell you about my little plan. I called Violet when I got back from the bank, and we came up with an exciting idea. I was telling her how much little Clarice looks like Mr. Merkin's daughter. We got to thinking that Mr. Merkin might like to see her. I mean, after all, he adored the child, so people say, and he's been alone ever since she disappeared. Violet and me got to thinking that he might be tickled to see a child there on the island just the way Caroline used to be. Just for a short visit, you know."

"But I thought he didn't allow anyone on his property," Aunt Doris said.

"Why, he doesn't! He doesn't! Usually, anyway. But we got to talking about it and thought, what if Clarice just showed up there? Surely he wouldn't chase away the spitting image of his own daughter! And he might find out that he enjoys seeing people again. Clarice could sort of break the ice, so to speak, she might lead the way so that other people might be allowed to visit on that island now and then. That's what Violet and me were talking about. And then Violet wouldn't have to be so lonely over there. Even if he still won't let other people visit the island, he might not raise a fuss 'bout me, because I would be the one who was there with the little girl who looked just like Caroline!'' Mrs. Quist beamed. ''So don't you think that's a wonderful plan?''

Aunt Doris frowned. ''But Clarice can't go over there, Edith! That's impossible.''

''No, no, not at all! Why, I'd take her there myself, Doris. I have a friend with a pontoon boat who'll be glad to take us over. Tonight! Violet said Mr. Merkin sits out on the back patio to watch the sunset in the evening, and he's all calm and relaxed. We could take the boat over and say hello and then hurry right on home again. It wouldn't have to be a long visit, you see. Just enough to open the door a bit. Violet gets so lonely, you know.''

''I'd like to go,'' Clarice said, bobbing closer in her inner tube.

''But it would be invading the man's privacy,'' Aunt Doris protested.

''Wouldn't it scare him?'' I asked. ''I mean, wouldn't it be like seeing a ghost?''

''How could he be scared of someone so much like his own child?'' Mrs. Quist stared at me. ''Why, he'd be glad, that's what I think. Tickled pink! I can get my friend to take us over in the boat, and we could be there and back in no time at all. It would certainly be a great favor to Violet. And to me, too, of course, to me, too.''

''Oh, I don't think so,'' Aunt Doris repeated. ''I—''

''But I want to go.'' Clarice carefully inched her inner tube onto the dock. She blinked her big blue eyes at Aunt Doris. ''I'd like to help Mrs. Quist and her friend. Mom always says we ought to help people when we can. Can't I go? Can't I go?''

She wasn't going to put one over on me. I shot forward. ''I'll bet Mom would let Clarice help Mrs. Quist and her friend, Aunt Doris. But she always tells us both to stick together, so I'd have to go, too.'' I tried to look uninterested but ready to carry out my duty. ''I don't mind going along.''

Clarice knew exactly what I was doing. Her ponytail swirled as she made a face at me, but Mrs. Quist was declaring her approval. ''That's a fine idea! A find idea! I can't imagine that Mr. Merkin would make a fuss if he sees two children, and one looks exactly like his long-lost Caroline. He'll be glad I brought them. I'd like to ask you to come along, too, Doris, but we don't want to upset the man. It'll be enough that two children and myself go visit his house. We wouldn't want to overwhelm him, you know. Oh, no, we wouldn't want to do that. We'll be there and back in no time at all. Now don't worry a single moment, dear, I'll make sure the girls have life jackets on when we're on the water. They'll be fine, just fine.''

''We'll be fine,'' I echoed. I tried to sound bored, but my head was spinning. I was actually going to get over there and walk right into the hazy mist of the island! Now I'd really see all the things I had been trying to imagine.

''I'd better get dressed.'' Clarice carefully placed her inner tube on the dock and climbed up. She brushed off her pink ruffled bathing suit, even though it was already spotless. ''Should I fix my hair like Caroline Merkin had her hair?'' she asked.

Mrs. Quist blinked at her. ''What? Oh no, dear. Your hair is fine just the way it is. It makes you look just the way Caroline Merkin looked all those years ago. The pictures showed a child just like you.'' Beaming, she stood up. ''Well, then, it's settled. I'll see about getting a boat set for us and drive the girls to the boat dock. Could we leave about seven o'clock? That'll give us a few hours of daylight, and it will be a good time for Mr. Merkin. Oh, I just feel certain he'll be glad to see visitors on the island this time.''

"We'll be ready," I said. "Right, Clarice?"

I could see that she still wasn't too pleased that I'd be going along, but she managed to nod.

Aunt Doris sighed. "I'm not sure this is a good idea," she mumbled. "But I guess it can't harm anyone if you're just going for a few moments. Let's get up to the cottage, girls, so I can think about getting something for you to eat before you leave."

"I'll just walk along the beach down here," Mrs. Quist told us. "Then I don't have to climb that awful hill. I'll be in front of the cottage just before seven. Oh, isn't this exciting! We'll be the first visitors Mr. Merkin has had in years!"

She didn't have to tell me that it would be exciting. I could hardly wait. I was feeling chills even though the sun was still hot.

Aunt Doris watched Mrs. Quist hurry away. "She sure gets caught up in her planning, doesn't she? She seemed so eager I hated to say no. I hope I haven't made a mistake."

Clarice patted her inner tube into the exact spot she used for it on the dock. "We're going to find out lots of new things, that's for sure." Then, when Aunt Doris bent to get her tanning lotions, she made a face at me. "Don't mention those pictures to Mrs. Quist! Detectives shouldn't tell everything they know."

I knew she was still bummed because I'd gotten myself invited on the trip to the island, too, so I inched closer to her and whispered her favorite words. "Nanny, nanny, boo, boo. I can do what you do!"

Surprises on the Island

Mrs. Quist's friend with a boat turned out to be Mr. Brock, from the grocery store. He sat up front, his long skinny body hunched around the boat controls, while we sat down on plastic seats along the railing. I tried to avoid looking at the bait bucket filled with worms that was under the seat. I'd had a fit about having to wear a big orange life jacket, but as soon as we reached the drop-off area, I was glad I had it on. The water there was so deep it looked pure black. It was exciting to be skimming over the top of the waves. Pontoons don't go fast as speedboats, but they go fast enough.

Mrs. Quist was sitting between Clarice and me. Her orange life jacket didn't quite stretch around her, and she looked nervous and uncomfortable. She nodded toward Mr. Brock. "I knew that Michael would be glad to take us. He's proud as a peacock over this new pontoon boat."

"Peacocks don't have anything to do with boats," Clarice said.

Mrs. Quist's mouth dropped open. She stared at Clarice a moment, maybe at a loss for words for the first time in her life. It's hard for other people to believe that Clarice thinks all words have to make absolute sense. Speaking words aloud to her is the same thing as writing them in cement. I felt so sorry for Mrs. Quist that I came to her rescue.

"Should we do anything special when we meet Mr. Merkin?"

She shook her head. "No, no, we'll just walk up to the house like ordinary guests, that's all. Violet will be on the patio having after-dinner coffee with Mr. Merkin. We figured it all out by telephone, and decided it was best not to warn him. He'll be surprised to see people on the island at first, of course, and he might be a little angry, Violet says. But since Clarice looks so much like Caroline, she's sure he won't stay mad. He'll be glad to see us, that's what Violet and I both think."

Clarice looked at Mr. Brock, busy steering his boat. "And will he come with us to the house, too?"

"Mercy no!" Mrs. Quist gasped in amazement at such a weird suggestion. "Three of us will be surprise enough! Violet's going to have Ronnie down by the dock because Michael wants to take him fishing. Ronnie will go back on the boat with us." She waved back behind us. "There's good fishing right at the rim of the drop-off back there in front of my cottages. Especially when it's just getting dark."

I stared back at the fading shoreline. Now it looked all hazy and mysterious by the shore where our cottage was hidden. The island, just ahead, looked bright and green. It seemed strange to me that things changed so much just because of how close or how far away you were from them.

As we drew closer to the island, I saw a long boat dock stretching out into the water. Ronnie was standing there waving. Mr. Brock lowered the motor power and waved back.

I kept looking around as I took off my life jacket and threw it onto the seat while Clarice neatly folded hers. Mr. Brock maneuvered the boat up beside the dock. Everything looked the same as it did on the other side of the lake. There were huge shrubs and trees along the shoreline. I felt a surge

of disappointment. Mysterious island life seemed just like plain old regular life.

Clarice and I both jumped off without having any trouble, but Ronnie and Mr. Brock had to help Mrs. Quist. "Don't let me fall," she kept saying, her face moist and red. "Why, I'd sink to the bottom like a rock!"

"Ma and him are out back," Ronnie said, when she was safely on the dock. He grinned and pushed at his Tigers cap. "I want to see, but Ma won't let me."

Mr. Brock patted him on the back. "We're going fishing—remember? Let's just walk along the shore here and see if we can get any worms for bait."

Mrs. Quist grabbed my arm. "We'll be back soon, Michael," she said, and she urged me and Clarice off the dock. She tried to sound brisk and efficient but I noticed that her voice wasn't nearly as booming as it usually was. We were all peering straight ahead. Like me, I guess Clarice and Mrs. Quist were wondering what Mr. Merkin would look like, what he might say or do.

There was a path leading through the trees by the shore, and as soon as we were on it, I saw the house. It was big and desolate, but it didn't resemble the house I had imagined we would find. I guess I had expected something scary, maybe something with bats and gigantic cobwebs like houses in horror movies. This house might have been on the cover of a home magazine. It was white with black shutters. The lawn was huge, all green and perfect, with sprinklers waving in all directions.

"Violet told me that her Henry keeps this lawn like a picture postcard," Mr. Quist said in a loud whisper. "And I see that she was right."

For some reason, I felt like whispering, too. It was the silence of the island that was doing it. Except for the sound of the sprinklers and the birds, everything was quiet. There was a huge porch stretching across the front of the house, but it was empty.

"The back patio must be out that way," Mrs. Quist said, pointing.

"I'll go first," Clarice said, moving ahead. She was dressed in white shorts and a white shirt. For once she'd left her ridiculous big purse at home. I had told her that a ghost wouldn't be caught dead carrying it. She hadn't seen the humor, but she'd agreed to leave it behind.

It was twilight now, and I wondered if Mr. Merkin would think he was seeing Caroline drifting across the shadows. I tried to slow my steps so that Clarice would be far out in front.

As we turned the corner to reach the back of the house, I saw two people in lawn chairs beside a table far ahead. A small, slender woman was facing us. She was peering in our direction with her face all wrinkled and worried. She saw us the same instant I saw her, so she jumped to her feet.

The other figure was sitting with his back toward us. I saw bushy gray hair and slouched shoulders. Then Mrs. Quist sort of pushed Clarice toward the figure. "We've come to visit," she boomed.

Violet Gallagher broke into a nervous smile and spoke at the very same moment. "Why look, Mr. Merkin. We have company."

I don't know what Clarice did or thought in that moment. I guess she was trying to look as much like Caroline Merkin as possible. I was just trying to look friendly as I met my first real live hermit. I pasted a huge smile on my face, not even caring that the sunburn hurt where the lines creased.

The slumping figure grew rigid at the sound of the voices, and then Mr. Merkin bolted from his chair. He whirled around in the same motion and stared directly at us.

He had a long skinny face with gray beard stubble. He glared at us through thick glasses while his amazed face puckered. And then—I know this is physically impossible, but it really did happen—every hair on his head seemed to stand out straight. Surprise turned to fury.

"Git!" he shouted, reaching for something on the table. "Git off my property! You hear me? Git off my property!" He flung back a long thin arm.

"But just look—" Mrs. Quist was waving her hands at Clarice. "She looks just like—"

A coffee cup came sailing past me. "Git!" Mr. Merkin shouted again, throwing his arm back for another pitch while Violet Gallagher stood paralyzed beside him. A saucer whizzed past Mrs. Quist. "Get out of here!"

We whirled around, all of us instantly convinced that he might pick up Violet and pitch her at us next. I grabbed Mrs. Quist's hand, and the two of us struggled out of the line of fire, Clarice right beside us.

"Don't ever come back!' Mr. Merkin shouted after us. "You hear me? You stay off my island! This here is private property!"

"Mercy!" Mrs. Quist was panting as we reached the path by the front of the house. "Mercy sakes! Mercy sakes!"

Violet came panting up behind us. "Oh my, I've never seen him so angry," she said. "Oh girls, I'm sorry! I'm sorry if he frightened you. But I really thought he'd be pleased to see the little girl."

Clarice smoothed down her long hair. She kept staring behind, as though afraid Mr. Merkin might still be pitching dishes.

Mrs. Quist had finally caught her breath. "Oh, Violet, I hope you haven't lost your job!"

"I'll go back and see if I can calm him down. Why, he

doesn't have to know I had anything to do with it, does he? But what a pity that he couldn't see that this girl looks so much like Caroline." She gave a quick shake of her head, then hurried on back up the path.

I was glad I wasn't the one who had to face Mr. Merkin. Clarice and I were thinking alike. At any minute I expected to see him flying around the pathway with more ammunition clutched in his hands. I jumped back onto the boat, but Mr. Brock and Michael were nowhere in sight. They didn't show up until Clarice and I had Mrs. Quist all settled on board again.

"What's going on?" Mr. Brock called as he and Ronnie came running. Mr. Brock threw an empty bucket under the plastic seats. "Wasn't the old man glad to see you?"

We were nearly halfway home by the time Mrs. Quist finished telling him what had happened. He whistled. "Too bad," he said. "Maybe his mind is gone after all these years of living alone. Oh well, Edith, you did your best to give him a bit of pleasure." They talked a bit more, but Ronnie started talking to me about his Tigers baseball cap, so I didn't hear. I was thinking about those pictures Mrs. Coles had shown us. Maybe Clarice wasn't a lookalike at all. Maybe the girl in those pictures was the real Caroline Merkin. I leaned over to tell Clarice.

"Mr. Merkin must not have thought you looked like his daughter at all. Do you suppose Carolyn Merkin was fat and dark-haired like the girl in those pictures we saw?"

"Maybe." Clarice was swinging her legs, and her words came in rhythm to the movements. "I asked Mrs. Quist where she saw those pictures. She said she can't remember."

I sighed. "From anybody else that would sound weird, but coming from her it sounds just about right." I leaned on the railing and looked out over the lake. By now darkness had fallen. A full moon was rising, and a few stars popped out of the darkness. The island was hidden in the shadows now. Mrs. Quist and Mr. Brock were talking about tomorrow's weather. "What a worthless trip," I mumbled.

Clarice shook her head. "I learned a lot, Flee Jay. Didn't you?"

I snorted. "I learned that you don't mess with hermits, that's for sure. And you don't try to bring back memories of someone who's been dead as a doornail for forty years. Why—what did you learn?"

She ignored me. Instead, she jumped up and moved closer to Mr. Brock. "Could my sister and I go fishing with you and Ronnie tonight? We think it'd be fun." My mouth dropped open when I heard the words. Clarice would never be able to touch a worm. And as far as I'm concerned, you get fish out of cans, and that's the best way to do it. I stared at her, but she waved her hand behind her back to tell me to be quiet.

"Nope." Mr. Brock gestured toward a cooler. "I've got a picnic here for just two. Ronnie and I will have a few beers, a few laughs. It's best that you girls get on home. Maybe I can take you fishing another time."

"I don't know *what* I'll tell their Aunt Doris," Mrs. Quist said, sighing. "She'll think I was a foolish old woman taking her nieces off on a wild-goose chase."

But Aunt Doris didn't think that at all. She said she was sorry we'd nearly been scared out of our wits. We sat in the cottage drinking lemonade while Mr. Quist apologized over and over. "It's just that I was sure he'd like seeing a child who looked so much like his daughter," she kept repeating. "I wish I could remember where I saw those pictures of Caroline, so I could show them to Violet."

Clarice stood up. "There's a pretty moon out tonight,

Aunt Doris. Would it be all right if Flee Jay and I went down by the lake for while?"

"Well—" Aunt Doris frowned. "I—"

"Oh, let them go," Mrs. Quist said. "If they cover themselves with some kind of bug stuff, they'll be fine. There's nothing that can hurt them down there, and it *is* a humdinger of a night, what with that full moon. Young girls need to be out under a full moon now and again. It makes them have curly hair." She laughed and patted her own curls. "Why, I've spent plenty of time in moonlight myself."

"Okay, then," Aunt Doris said. "But curly hair wouldn't much matter to either of these girls. I didn't realize that you two were so interested in the moon, Clarice."

I hadn't realized it either, but as soon as we were dressed in our jeans and sweatshirts, I followed Clarice from the cottage. She was carrying her big purse and it was bulging more than usual. I knew she wanted to do more than just watch the moon. "You'd better have a good reason for dragging me off down this hill again," I whispered to her.

She blinked her innocent blue eyes at me. "Why, we're just going to look at the moon!" she said, running ahead. She laughed and called back, "Besides, you want curly hair, don't you?"

She knew very well I hated my frizzy hair. I frowned and followed her down the hill, wishing the moonlight would frizzle hers.

Moonlight Horror

Refusing to answer any questions, Clarice hurried the rest of the way down the hill and to the end of the dock. It seemed strange to be there in the darkness. Our footsteps sounded lonely and hollow on the wooden planks.

The moon was hanging low in the sky. Huge dark clouds kept drifting across its face, hiding it completely, throwing everything below into eerie shadows. Far up beyond them, the moon glowed in the blackness, but Clarice ignored it, just as I had known she would. She had as much interest in studying the sky as a flea has in studying the anatomy of a dog.

I looked all around and felt a sense of gloom. In the trees behind us, the lonely hoot of an owl echoed across the air. Magic Lake stretched out in front of us, silent and dark.

The only sign of life was Mr. Brock's pontoon boat anchored just at the rim of the drop-off far out in front of us. Lights at each end of the deck moved in a rhythmic pattern as the boat bobbed up and down. The people on board were hidden in the darkness, but every now and again I could hear the murmur of voices, Mr. Brock's deep, rumbly one, and Ronnie Gallagher's high, excited one.

"So?" I whispered. "What was the big deal about getting me down here?

Clarice pointed at the boat. "I want to know what they're talking about out there, Flee Jay. I'm beginning to get an idea of what's happening, and I need to hear what they're talking about in order to be sure."

I heaved a great sigh. I was getting cold, and the bugs were buzzing around me. Just like beauty products, insect repellents fail once they're rubbed on me. My poison ivy felt itchy. "You got me down here for that? They're probably talking about a ball game!"

Clarice shook her head. "Oh, I think they're talking about something more than a ball game. I'm going to find out for sure, and I may need your help. If I hear what they're talking about, maybe I'll have some answers to a few puzzles." She reached down to take off her jeans. "I'm going to go for a little moonlight swim."

I caught my breath. "Out over that drop-off? No way! You're a good swimmer, Clarice, but nobody's *that* good. Besides, you know I can't swim. I couldn't help you even if you were drowning."

She dropped her sweatshirt onto the dock, and I saw that she had had her bathing suit on under her clothes. "I won't need to be way out over the drop-off. I'll just get close enough to the boat to hear voices. Sound travels far on water."

I glared at her even though I knew it was far too dark for her to see my face. Emotion between sisters travels far, too, and you don't need water to carry it. "But they'd see you when the moon is clear again. And they'd hear you splashing. Even if they *did* plan to talk about something important, they aren't going to say anything with you thrashing around out there."

"Yes, they will. Because they won't know I'm there." She sat down and neatly folded her clothes. "I've got this good idea, Flee Jay."

And so that's when she told me her great plan. Her idea was really scary, and I told her so. But trying to get Clarice to forget one of her schemes by using words is like trying to stop Niagara Falls from flowing by throwing a cup of water at it. She had a lot more words than I did. Also—I have to be honest—I was just as curious as she was about what they were talking about. Mr. Brock had made it plain that he wanted to be alone with Ronnie on that boat. And I'd noticed another funny thing. He had said that he wanted Ronnie to help him find worms on the island for bait, but I had seen a bucketful of worms on board the pontoon. I wondered if Clarice had noticed that, too. I thought it might be a clue to something, but I couldn't think what, and I wanted to wait to talk about it until I had some kind of idea.

"I'll just float off in the inner tube," she told me, her voice all breathless. "Most of me will be down under the water. Only my head will be up, and it will be hidden by the rim of the inner tube. It'll look just like the tube accidently floated away from the dock. You stay right here. I'll tell you what to say to make it seem more real."

And so I found myself shouting into the darkness just a few moments later. As clouds rolled across the moon, I screamed, "See you later, Clarice. I'm going to stay down here on the dock awhile longer," as though she had climbed the hill to the cottage.

In the meantime, she climbed into the larger inner tube and silently slipped away.

I felt pretty silly right then, more embarrassed than scared. I felt as though she and I were actresses putting on a show in an empty theater.

After I delivered my big speech, I plopped down on the edge of the dock again. Then I was sorry that I'd been in such a big hurry, because a sliver rammed into the skin on the back of my leg. By the time I pulled that out, the clouds had passed, and I saw the silhouettes bobbing on the silent water.

There was the pontoon boat again, but now, floating on a path in its direction, was the inner tube. It looked empty and innocent, and its steady movement was so slight that it looked as though the current alone was moving it along.

The thought of that current and the deep water over that drop-off just ahead sent chills racing up my spine. Suddenly I wanted to shout out to Clarice to come back, to forget all about her crazy plan for eavesdropping.

But instead I just sat there with my heart pounding, while the tube drifted silently into deeper water. I was scared to shout and scared not to shout.

More clouds passed across the moon, and the night was pitch black again. I could only see faint glimmers from the lanterns on the pontoon boat. It seemed a long, long way off, and it seemed to be rocking faster now. The waves had picked up rhythm. They were slapping harder against the dock below me.

I inched forward on the dock, willing the clouds away so that I could see the safety of that inner tube and know that Clarice was all right. As soon as the moonlight pierced through the blackness again, I saw it. The tube was bouncing just a few yards off the side of the boat.

"Hey kid!"

I jumped to my feet as Mr. Brock's voice came bounding over the water.

"That your tube?" he yelled.

Clarice had told me exactly what to say in case the inner tube was noticed. I cupped my hands around my mouth. "It's okay," I shouted. "Guess it floated away. It'll float back."

"I'll help it along!" he shouted, and before I could open my mouth again, I saw the silhouette of his fishing pole sail back and out again.

"He got it!" Ronnie called, and I saw the outline of both men bend down. They pulled the tube closer to the boat.

I clenched my fists. My stomach knotted as I imagined the fish hooks zinging through Clarice's hair inside that tube. My fingernails dug into my palms. I told myself that she must have ducked down in time, that she was perfectly fine. Soon her head would spring to the surface, and she would tell the men that she'd been playing a joke. But I couldn't see a trace of her, couldn't see even a tiny movement in the water no matter how I squinted and peered.

"I'll toss this as hard as I can," Mr. Brock shouted.

I jumped into the water to shout back. If Clarice was still okay and hiding, she would need the tube to reach shore again without them seeing her. But I didn't even get my mouth open in time to stop him. The shock of feeling that cold water was nothing compared to the shock of hearing the smack of that inner tube hitting the water out past the dock in front of me.

"You can get it now," Ronnie called.

I stood shivering, looking at the empty tube as it bobbed in the water. I looked beyond it, but there wasn't a single speck on the still water. Surely Clarice had to come to the surface to breathe. But where was she? Where was she?

I went racing through the knee-deep waves, splashing water in all directions. I was so scared my brain was spinning as I grabbed it. "Clarice?" I whispered foolishly, peering inside.

But it was empty, of course. The lake had absorbed the movement and sound, and now it was as silent as death again. I squinted my eyes and tried to peer through the shadows. The men on the boat were quiet again, and only calm ripples marred the surface of the water. I stared harder, eager to see the speck of Clarice's head somewhere between me and the boat. If she were still alive, she would have to breathe, she would have to surface somewhere.

But there wasn't a sign of her. The night went black again. I stood there clutching that inner tube, visualizing Clarice sinking deeper and deeper into the currents of that huge black drop-off. She had disappeared as completely as Mrs. Merkin, as completely as Caroline. My thoughts hammered in wild rhythm to the thumping of my heart, and I knew I needed to get help. I started running into deeper water, screaming to Mr. Brock.

But at the same instant, the pontoon motor burst into life, and more lights flashed on the boat. Panting, I screamed louder, but no one on board could hear me calling now. Tears blurred my vision as I saw the boat turn and move back toward Merkin Island.

Moaning, I shivered in the cold water and hugged the empty tube tighter, waiting for a miracle, waiting to see Clarice spring to the surface, even though I knew no one could live that long without breathing. Right that moment I changed my whole way of thinking about her. I hated myself for ever being nasty to Clarice, and I vowed that if I ever had another chance, I would always be kind and loving. I would never be angry at her again, not ever. "Not ever," I whispered out loud as all my fear and terror melted into sorrow.

My throat ached. How would I ever tell Aunt Doris? How would I ever tell my parents? Maybe it would be better to walk out into the drop-off myself, I thought. It would be easier to do that than to admit that I had let my sister drown.

Secret Hiding Place

Sometimes when you want something really a lot, you can wish for it so hard that you imagine you actually have it. That's the way it was when I heard a slight splashing in the water out beyond the dock. It was too dark for me to see, but I clenched my fists and caught my breath, willing it to be Clarice, even though I knew it was impossible. I tried not to breathe again, so that I could listen more carefully, afraid that I had only imagined the sound.

But I heard it again. "Clarice?" I shouted. "Clarice?" Clutching the tube, I tried to run deeper into the water as the clouds uncovered the moon. Someone was swimming toward shore!

Clarice's voice vibrated over the water. "I'm okay!"

In seconds I was grabbing her, hardly even caring that my clothes were wringing wet.

She was laughing and spitting out water. "I swam under their boat and hid. In that hollow place between the two pontoons. So I could hear them better. I had to be real quiet so they wouldn't hear me in there. There wasn't any way I could let you know I was okay."

My emotions were churning. All of the affection and fear I had felt before exploded into anger. Just seconds before I had been praying that she would be alive, and now I suddenly felt

like killing her. I pushed her away. "You scared me nearly to death!" I shouted. "I ought to strangle you. I ought to cut you up into a zillion pieces!"

Clarice splashed on over to the dock. I heard her open that ugly purse of hers, and as I moved in closer, she leaned over and handed me a towel. "Here. Use this, Flee Jay. You'll feel better."

I gasped. "You had a *towel* in there?"

"Sure. I knew I'd need it." She leaned closer. "But I didn't know that *you* would need it. I'm sorry, Flee Jay. Really I am. I know you must have been scared, but I didn't know what else to do. I had to hide under there, otherwise they would have seen me. There wasn't any way I could let you know. And when Mr. Brock sent his fishhook into the tube, I was glad I was out of there. I'm sorry it scared you so much, though."

I buried my face in the towel. It smelled like the disinfectant Clarice always carries in her purse. "I wasn't scared or worried *at all!*" I told her. "Not one bit!"

As I climbed on the dock, I noticed that I still had my shoes on. "Look at me," I wailed. "Aunt Doris is going to have a fit!"

"I'm sorry," Clarice said again. She took the towel and mopped her face. "Want to wrap my jeans around you? They're nice and dry."

"No." The moon was hidden again, and the darkness was wet and cold. I stood up, and the water in my shoes squished as I took a few steps. "Let's just get back to the cottage. Sure hope Mrs. Quist has left. I don't feel like answering a bunch of questions."

Clarice pulled her sweatshirt over her head. She hopped into her jeans. I could tell that she was trying to be on her best behavior, but I still wasn't sure whether I should kiss her or kill her. "And did you find out anything after all this?" I asked. "Did you hear them talk about anything that can help us figure out what's going on?"

She flapped her towel, then carefully folded it for her purse. "I heard things. But nothing made any sense. Mr. Brock wants something Ronnie has. He kept asking where 'it' was."

"But what could Ronnie have that's worth anything?"

Clarice shrugged as she pushed back her wet hair. "I have one idea, but it doesn't much matter. Looks like Ronnie has hidden this thing where nobody will find it anyway. None of his answers made any sense to Mr. Brock—or to me either."

We were walking up the hill now, and I felt as soggy and as helpless as a wet paper doll. If Clarice couldn't figure something out, it seemed a sure thing that *I* couldn't. I marched along, dripping and squishing with every step. My poison ivy itched. Mosquitoes buzzed around my head, and mud collected on my shoes. The whole evening had ended in failure.

"All our plans tonight have fizzled," I said, "starting with Mr. Merkin. He didn't care one bit that you looked like his daughter."

Clarice's voice was soft in the darkness. "I don't think I do."

"Well, I've been thinking the same thing. But why would Mr. Brock and Mrs. Quist both say that you look just like her?"

"Maybe they just wanted to use me as an excuse to get on the island. That's what I've been thinking, Flee Jay."

"They didn't do anything on the island. Mrs. Quist was with us the whole time. And Mr. Brock and Ronnie only went to look for—" I stopped, suddenly remembering the bait already on board.

"They didn't need bait," Clarice finished for me. "Guess you noticed that, too. It looked to me like Mr. Brock wanted to be alone with Ronnie on the island shore. Maybe he doctored up some old pictures to show Mrs. Quist or something. Somehow he convinced her that I looked just like Caroline Merkin so that she'd take me there and use his boat. Maybe he thought that Ronnie had hidden 'it' there."

"But why would Mrs. Quist go along with that idea? She's so—so—"

"I don't know what to think about her, Flee Jay. She says she doesn't remember where she saw the pictures she talked about. She's such a flutterbrain, I guess she *could* forget, but what if Mr. Brock just told her to say that? And what about those pictures Mrs. Coles had? Is that really what Caroline Merkin looked like? Who wrote the name? What about the vandals? Did they really take them? How come? There are too many questions here, Flee Jay, that's the trouble. And none of the questions lead to logical answers. I thought maybe I'd hear something on that boat that would help, but nothing made any sense there either."

I peered at Clarice's face, all speckled with leaf shadows as we walked along in the moonlight. "So what exactly did they talk about?" I asked.

"Mr. Brock kept telling Ronnie to eat or drink a little more, and then he'd laugh and say, 'Come on, come on, Ronnie, tell me where it is.' Then Ronnie would laugh and say something, 'Secret. Can't tell.' That doesn't help at all!"

We were almost to the top of the hill. I saw the lights of our cottage flickering in the distance. A light along the path flashed huge shadows at us. I waved away a few bugs and plodded on.

"The only place Ronnie mentioned doesn't make any sense," Clarice went on. "Snake Tree. He said something about Snake Tree. But it didn't mean any more to Mr. Brock than it does to me. How could a tree be a snake?"

I stopped so fast Clarice banged right into me. Triumph all warm and prickly went surging through my body. I grabbed her arm. "*I* know what Snake Tree is! I even know where it is!"

She blinked up at me. "You do?"

And so while she stared at me, I told her all about that tree in the cove where I'd splashed water on my poison ivy during our first trip to the store. "The roots are all tangled up like a bunch of snakes," I said. "You have to be sitting right on the shore to see it, though. I'll bet most adults wouldn't even notice it."

Clarice was grinning and nodding. "Ronnie would see it, though. He's always back in the bushes and trees along the shoreline. That's it, Flee Jay! Let's go see if we can find something special by that tree. Let's go!"

I looked down at my soggy clothes. "But we've got to get to the cottage now, Clarice. It's late. And Aunt Doris would never let us go anywhere else tonight."

Clarice frowned. "Let's not ask, then. If we don't ask her, she can't tell us we can't go."

"But she'll worry if we don't get home soon." My voice rose. "And I'm wringing wet! We've got to—"

"Shhhhhh!" Clarice turned toward the cottage. "I mean that we'll go later. After Aunt Doris is asleep. I'll tell my brain to wake me up at 4 A.M. And then I'll wake you up."

"But can't we go tomorrow at a decent time?"

"No. Somebody might see us go there in the daylight. We've got to go while it's still dark."

"You mean we should just go sneaking out in the middle of the night?"

"Sure."

All the years of my parents telling me that I was older than Clarice so I was supposed to watch over her thundered in my head. "Well, my gosh, Clarice, I don't think that—"

"I'll go alone, then."

"But it might be nothing! We don't even know what Ronnie's hidden away, for gosh sakes! I mean, we could go down to that tree and find that Ronnie has hidden away a pretty flower or some dumb thing. Maybe there's another place that looks like a snake, and we'd end up running around in the middle of the night for nothing."

I took a deep breath. "Besides, what about those vandals? Maybe they'll be running around loose tonight, too. And who'll be out at that hour if we get in trouble?"

"Okay, don't go then. I'll go alone."

"What if something happens? Kids can't go tromping around in the middle of the night. What if Aunt Doris caught us? She'd blame me, that's what, because I'm older. I'm trying to be sensible here, Clarice."

"Just stay home, then. You don't need to come along with me."

I could tell by her tone of voice that Clarice was really going to go by herself. With her luck, she'd find something wonderful by Snake Tree, and she'd get all the credit.

I grabbed her arm. "Oh, what the heck. I'll go with you. I'm the one who thought of Snake Tree, didn't I? So go ahead and set that perfect alarm clock in your head."

I didn't add any more words aloud, but in my mind, I added, "But I'm doing this against my better judgment." It seemed to me that we'd already taken enough chances for one night.

On the other hand, Snake Tree might have all the answers we were looking for. And hadn't I been the one who came up with the big clue? I planned to remind Clarice of who thought of it if we found something there. "Don't forget to wake me," I whispered as we opened up the screen door of the cottage.

Buried Treasure

Magic Lake Road was as dark and silent as a tomb. The moon was completely hidden now, and no stars were visible. No lamps shone from windows of the cottages hidden in the trees and there were no streetlights. No trucks pulling boats went zooming past, no mopeds or motorcycles roared along beside us. At four o'clock in the morning, the whole area was deserted. Clarice and I moved along in the blackness. I was still half asleep, grumpy, and—although I wasn't going to admit it to Clarice—scared.

There were noises coming from the darkness beside the road—strange sounds that gave me the creeps. There was a rustling and a rushing in the bushes, a fluttering and flapping among the tree leaves, and always, like a steady heartbeat, the sound of the lake waves slapping against the shore far off to the right of us.

I shivered as I walked along, as much from the spooky eeriness as from the cold. My jeans and sweatshirt covered my pajamas, but my thoughts gave me chills. First of all, I wondered what we might find when we got to Snake Tree. Then I wondered what Aunt Doris would do if she woke up and found us gone. Then my head whirled with wondering whether that peculiar tree I had noticed was really the Snake Tree Ronnie had talked about.

Then that idea gave me an even scarier worry. I wondered if snakes ever crawled along the roadside in the middle of the night. I nudged Clarice. "Can't you flash that lantern on for just a little while?"

Clarice quickly shifted the boat lantern to her other hand. It was made to look like an old oil lantern from an ancient ship, but it was really brand-new, and it used batteries instead of oil. Mrs. Quist had them by every cottage door.

"We'll need this for later," Clarice answered, "when we get to that creek. We might have to search all over down there, and I don't know how good the batteries are in this."

"It probably has more energy than I do," I mumbled, trudging along. After a few more moments, I spoke my fear aloud. "Sure hope that Ronnie's Snake Tree is the same as mine. I'd hate to think we're heading in the wrong direction."

"I think we're on the right track, Flee Jay. Remember where we saw Ronnie for the first time?"

"Sure. It was right along this road. So what?"

"Well, maybe he was coming from his secret hiding place near the creek right then. He'd been walking down by water just a few minutes before we saw him. His shoes had fresh mud. Didn't you notice that?"

I hadn't. "Well, sure. But that doesn't prove anything. He might have just been wading in the lake."

"With his shoes on? No, logic tells you that people don't do that."

I felt my own damp feet. "People have wet shoes for lots of reasons. Let's face it, Clarice. Logic doesn't help in some cases. Look at us. We're marching along in the middle of the night and we don't know whether we're going to the right place, and we don't know what it is we're looking for."

She sniffed. "I know. I know exactly what we're looking for."

I stopped in midstride. "What? What'd you say?"

"I know what Ronnie hid. At least I'm ninety-nine and forty-four one-hundredths percent sure."

I nearly tripped over my wet shoelaces. "You're putting me on! How could you know?"

"I just use logic." Clarice skipped ahead of me. "I figured it out by thinking what we saw and heard. When I looked over all my notes and put the clues together, I knew what we'd have to look for." She stopped and called back. "You would know, too, if you thought about it, Flee Jay. Just put all the clues together."

"Then you heard more than you told me. When you were eavesdropping, you heard more than you said."

"Nope. I told you everything I heard. But I've put the ideas from the last three days together, and now I see a clear picture. I know what we're looking for. I don't know how valuable it is, but I know what it is."

I bit my lip. Even though I had sprained my brain, I still didn't have the slightest idea of what Ronnie might have hidden.

"It's because I notice things, Flee Jay," Clarice went on. "I look at everything around me, and I think about it. You look at things, but you don't *see* what you're looking at. Nanny, nanny, boo,boo—you can't do what I do!"

As she called those last lines, she darted ahead. Obviously she was no longer on her best behavior. Shoving my hands in my pockets, I followed her, vowing to come up with an answer. What could Ronnie have hidden that Mr. Brock wanted?

I thought about all the times we had seen him, because every time Clarice had seen him, I'd been there, too. Except for being under the boat. But she had told me everything she heard, so that didn't count.

We'd seen Mr. Brock in his store the first day, and we'd seen him again on the boat. But he'd never talked about any kind of treasure. In fact, he'd hardly mentioned Ronnie's name at all. We saw Ronnie beside the road, but it seemed to me that Mrs. Quist had done all the talking there. What clues could Clarice have heard or seen that I hadn't? I watched Clarice's ghostly figure jumping around ahead of me, and my brain was as blank as the road. I ran to catch up with her. I was determined to be right by her side when she started searching around Snake Tree.

Fifteen minutes later, we came to the small creek. I could hear the water gurgling far into the deep blackness. Clarice switched on the lantern. As we walked down the hill to the lake, an insect chirped, but at the sudden blast of light, it grew quiet. The two of us inched our way forward.

There was a damp earthly smell, and I thought it was exactly like the smell in a snake house at a zoo. Twigs snapped under our weight, and the noise vibrated in the stillness. I pressed my lips together, determined not to ask Clarice whether snakes crawled around at night. I was glad I had thick socks and jogging shoes on, even if they were damp and muddy.

The trees all looked bleak and grasping in the lantern light. The ferns, more than waist-high, sent shadows leaping ahead of us. Bushes blocked our way and pulled at our clothes. The small sloping hill seemed steeper and longer than I remembered.

Then we were at the bottom, where the creek trickled into the lake.

Clarice flashed the light over the roots of the large tree near the shoreline. I caught my breath. "That's it!" In the moving brightness, the roots of the tree looked tangled, brown, and bare, exactly like a heap of angry snakes.

I ran ahead and fell to my knees. "Do you think he hid something under one of the roots here?" As I spoke I poked my fingers in and out.

"Be careful of real snakes under there," Clarice whispered.

I jumped to my feet, threw my muddy hands to my face. Then I noticed that Clarice was laughing. "Snakes don't live in mud," she said, giggling.

But her giggles soon turned to sighs as we continued to poke around.

We found absolutely nothing. There were only rocks and sticks wedged under the tree roots. I felt cold and damp with disappointment.

"Could there be a hole in the tree somewhere?" I asked, running my hands around the tree trunk. But there was no hollow spot, no opening at all.

"Hey, look at this," Clarice called from behind me. "Looks like someone moved this rock recently."

She was crouched by the tangle of tree roots, a large rock at her feet.

I leaped forward and turned it over. I caught my breath. There was a small plastic package lying in the dirt beneath it.

"A bread wrapper?" I asked, bending closer.

Clarice picked it up. "Of course. Remember when Mrs. Quist told us about the missing bread wrapper? I thought we'd find it here. But there's something special inside here, Flee Jay, and I know what that is, too." As she talked, she unraveled the long plastic bag. I leaned forward, expecting money or jewels to fall out. Shadows were darting in the flickering light.

"Hurry up!" I cried, as Clarice finally reached the end.

It was only a small piece of cardboard. I slumped. "It's nothing!" I said.

"It's more than nothing!" Clarice grabbed the lantern and flashed it near the cardboard. I saw six figures, and three of them were $100,000.

Clarice grinned at me. "It's a lottery ticket, Flee Jay. Just what I thought." She looked back down at it. "I was pretty sure that's what it would be. But I never dreamed it was worth *that* much."

"My gosh." I kept staring at the small ticket. It was colored silver and green, and it had a picture of the state of Michigan across the top. There were six figures, and the rules said that if three figures were identical, the person turning in the ticket would win that amount of money. Three of them on this ticket were $100,000. "Gosh," I said again. "I don't think Ronnie could know how much money this is."

"But Mr. Brock knows," Clarice said. She leaned back on her heels. "Because Ronnie bought it from him. I figured that out when I remembered how he sold lottery tickets in his store. Ronnie's old enough to buy them, even though he can't know what they mean. When that bread wrapper disappeared, I was pretty sure Ronnie had put a lottery ticket in it. That had to be the treasure Mr. Brock was trying to get back."

All the clues fit together all right. My skin crawled as I looked at Clarice. The shadows danced around us, and my stomach churned. "Mr. Brock couldn't have done it all alone," I said. "Somebody had to help him. His store sold the ticket, so someone else would have to go to Lansing to claim it."

"And I guess we both know who had to be working with him," Clarice answered. Slumping, she turned to move back up to the road again.

I opened my mouth to answer, but the words stuck in my

throat. We both stopped dead in our tracks. There was a movement in the darkness. The shadow of a man darted into the circle of light from our lantern. I grabbed Clarice's arm. "Somebody's there! Somebody's been listening!"

Instantly she turned off the light. Hardly daring to breathe, we stood trembling in the darkness.

The Confession

Time goes more slowly when it's dark. We stood clutching each other for what seemed like hours, but I guess it was really only seconds. Then we heard footsteps rustling in the dead leaves. I breathed again when I realized that the noises were moving away from us, heading back through the trees to the cottages farther down by the lake.

"He's gone!" I whispered. "Who was it, Clarice? Do you think—"

"It was Mr. Brock," Clarice whispered back. "I'm sure of it. He must have been coming in from fishing when he saw our light."

"But why didn't he say anything? Why didn't he do anything?"

Clarice flicked on the light again. Holding it up high, she glanced all around. "I don't know. But I'm pretty sure he's gone. That's all I care about. Let's go!"

We didn't say much as we half-jogged, half-ran along the highway. My head was spinning with thoughts of why Mr. Brock had simply walked away. And my stomach was aching with thoughts of Mrs. Quist. She was the only one who could have helped Mr. Brock, and we both knew it. The idea didn't make me feel very happy. Even though Mrs. Quist was sort of a flutterbrain, I still couldn't help liking her. Clarice was so quiet that I was sure she felt the same way.

"Sometimes it isn't much fun coming up with the right answers," she finally mumbled, panting as we ran.

"So there's more than just plain logic to answers. Right?" I asked, but she only ran faster through the early dawn.

We saw Mrs. Quist's porch light burning when we turned into the cottage driveway. A figure waved to us from the porch. "Girls, girls!" Mrs. Quist whispered into the stillness. "Come in, please come in. Michael called me. He said you know everything. I want to explain. Want to—"

"He scared us to death!" I said as we hurried through her door.

"Michael wouldn't have hurt you! Oh no, girls, no, no, not at all." Her face looked frightened in the glaring porch light, and she looked old and tired without any makeup on. "Michael said we might as well tell the whole story now. Believe me, neither of us wanted to hurt anybody. Neither of us wanted that!" She pointed us toward the kitchen and sank into a chair.

Clarice put the lamp on the table. "You and Mr. Brock tried to cheat Ronnie."

Mrs. Quist closed her eyes. "So you really *do* know everything, then. Well, I'm glad, that's what! I'm glad! I'm glad this whole business is over! I'm sorry I got into this awful mess." She sighed. "But it seemed so harmless in the beginning."

She glanced at the window. Birds were chattering in the pine trees, but I soon forgot their noise and I only heard Mrs. Quist's voice.

"I was in the store last week when Ronnie came in to buy a few things for Violet. He had a few dollars left, so Michael asked if he wanted to buy a lottery ticket. Ronnie knows nothing about lotteries, of course, but he handed over a dollar and took the ticket. It was a joke, don't you know. Sort of a joke. All of us up here buy those tickets all the time. Nobody ever wins much, but we all keep hoping for the big jackpot. And there it was! One hundred thousand dollars was written three times on Ronnie's ticket! Michael and I were nearly bowled over. Nearly bowled over."

She pulled a handkerchief out of her robe pocket and wiped her face. "But it didn't mean a thing to Ronnie. Not a thing. Why, he couldn't even sign his name on the back, the way you're supposed to do! But he hung on to it for dear life. He liked the picture on the ticket, he said. That was all he noticed."

"And Mr. Brock saw how much it was worth, too?" Clarice asked.

Mrs. Quist's eyes flooded with tears. "Girls, I don't think you can understand this, but I've been desperate for money the past month. Building these extra cottages was a big mistake. The bank was calling for money, and I didn't know what to do. Michael is in the same fix. His store has been losing money for months. So we saw right away that the lottery winnings could save us both. Without doing any real harm, I mean. We thought we could get Ronnie to hand his ticket over to me. Then I could go to Lansing to cash it, and I could share the money with Michael." Her face grew even more serious. "And I'll tell you something, even though you might not believe it. I was going to be sure that some of my share of the money went to Violet. Money doesn't mean anything to Ronnie, but I knew it would mean a lot to her."

She stared out the window. "Well, sir, we tried everything we could think of to get that ticket away from Ronnie. We couldn't just grab it, now could we? He might have raised a real ruckus, and then what would we have done? So Michael offered him candy. I offered to buy him ten or even a hundred more of the same tickets with the same picture. But Ronnie wouldn't hear of it. He didn't know the value of that lottery ticket, but he wasn't going to let go of it for love nor money. It just didn't seem fair. Not a bit fair. I might have bought that ticket myself that day. I buy lottery tickets all the time."

She wiped her face again. "Well, when he left the store with it, we thought it was all over. We were sure he was going to give it to his mother or his father. He would know what the lottery winning meant, sure as shooting! I called Violet later that day, but she never mentioned the ticket. She only said that—"

"That her bread wrapper was missing," Clarice finished. "So you figured Ronnie had probably used it to wrap up the ticket and hide it."

"That's right! That's right! So Michael and I thought we still had a chance." Her face crumpled. She bit her lip. "Oh my stars, this sounds so awful, girls! But we never meant to harm anyone. We never meant for things to get out of hand. And I never suspected that Michael would—" She wiped her face, took a deep breath, and started in again.

"We decided Ronnie had buried it near the boat dock on the island, so we knew Michael had to get over there with Ronnie somehow. He thought Ronnie might show him exactly where the package was buried if he was right there with him. But we needed to have a reason why Michael was there with his boat."

"So Mr. Brock made up the 'lookalike' story," Clarice said.

"I'd told him that a ten-year-old was coming with Doris this year," she went on, "and that started it. We planned to pretend that you looked just like the lost Caroline Merkin."

"So you never really saw any pictures?" I asked. "You made up that whole thing about seeing a ghost when you first saw Clarice?"

Mrs. Quist looked at her hands. "I had to make your aunt believe that story so that she'd let Clarice go to the island. Don't you see how one thing depended on the other? But really I was afraid that I couldn't really make anyone believe I thought I'd seen a ghost. I've never been much of an actress. When I jumped up, though, my chair tipped over and it nearly scared the wits out of me. I guess my face looked as surprised as if I truly had seen that lost child. I guess I fooled everybody."

"We were fooled then all right," Clarice agreed. "But later I knew you'd lied. You said that I looked just like those pictures when my hair was hanging. Then later, on the dock, you said I looked just like those pictures when my hair was in a ponytail. That's when I was sure you hadn't seen any pictures at all. But I still wondered about Mr. Brock's story. When Mr. Merkin didn't recognize me, I knew that you both had lied."

"My stars!" Mrs. Quist declared. "I nearly was scared out of my wits when that man started tossing things at us! I never dreamed he'd do that to a child! I figured that even if you didn't look like his daughter, he'd still be glad to see you because of your age and all. And I guess I hoped maybe you did look like Caroline Merkin a little bit. I wanted to give Michael time with Ronnie, don't you know."

"Mr. Brock made up all that stuff about being Caroline Merkin's friend, didn't he?" I said, beginning to get an idea.

Mrs. Quist nodded. "Yes, we planned that he'd do that so your aunt would know that at least two of us saw the resemblance between you and Caroline Merkin. But Michael went ahead and did some things I never knew he would do. He went a lot farther than I ever guessed he would."

"He broke into Mrs. Coles's store," I blurted because suddenly I knew my idea was the truth.

Mrs. Quist gasped. "You know that, too?"

Clarice blinked at me. I could see she was as surprised as Mrs. Quist was that I had guessed the answer. "I was pretty sure all along," she said. "Someone was outside the door when Mrs. Coles was telling us about those old pictures of Caroline Merkin. When the store was vandalized, only those pictures were gone. I decided that the whole purpose of the break-in was to make those pictures disappear. After we found the lottery ticket, I figured out the rest of this. Mr. Brock seemed the logical suspect." She glanced at me again. "Flee Jay and I both came up with the same answer."

"My stars," Mrs. Quist said, staring from Clarice to me and then back again. Her face flushed. "You girls are almost like detectives! But listen! I never knew Michael was going to do that, girls. No sir, I wouldn't have gone along with that! I really did think Marie's store had been vandalized by a bunch of hooligans. I called him last night when he got home from fishing, and I told him I thought we should give up on this whole business. When he told me he had broken into Marie's store and stolen those pictures, I was fit to be tied. I would never go along with a break-in. No, no, never, never. We could go to jail for that!"

"People go to jail for fraud, too," Clarice said. "For what you were doing to Ronnie."

"But I didn't hurt anyone," Mrs. Quist said. Her eyes were all teary again. "And I was going to share the money with his mother. Don't forget that."

She was still reminding us of that fact when we left. "Tell your aunt all about this," she called after us. "I'll be here. I don't know where Michael will be, but I'll be here. I'm sorrier than the dickens about all this, you know. Sorrier than the dickens!"

I didn't feel very cheerful as we hurried to our own cottage. "What do you think Aunt Doris will say?" I asked.

"I guess she'll say we have to call the police or something," Clarice said, and I could see she felt as bad as I did. "Rats! It's fun to catch a villain, but it's no fun catching somebody you like."

"You can say that again," I told her.

"It's fun to catch a villain," she began, but I stopped her before she repeated the whole thing. Like I've said before, Clarice believes words mean exactly what they say.

"I heard you the first time," I mumbled. "Come on, let's go wake up Aunt Doris."

Amazing Answers

"Oh my goodness!" Aunt Doris kept saying as she stared at the lottery ticket. "Oh my goodness!"

Clarice and I ate breakfast while we told her everything that had happened. Clarice got to talk the most because I was hungrier.

"So when I was under the pontoon boat last night, I heard Mr. Brock say—"

"But I figured out what Snake Tree meant," I interrupted, because it was beginning to sound like Clarice had done *all* the detecting.

"Under the pontoon!" Aunt Doris shrieked.

It took a long time to get the whole story out, but finally Aunt Doris knew it all. "But of course I'll have to call the police," she said. "Oh my goodness, what a mess!"

"Will Mrs. Quist have to go to jail?" I asked.

"I don't know the answer to that, honey." Aunt Doris sighed. "The lottery ticket belongs to the Gallaghers, of course. If they press charges, there will be an investigation. Mr. Brock broke into Mrs. Coles's store. She might want to sign a formal complaint. And I suppose that Mr. Merkin has reason to complain about trespassers on his property. Oh my goodness! Well, I'll call the police and let them sort it all out."

"I'll go down and tell Mrs. Coles," Clarice said. "She'd be at her store now, and her phone isn't connected there yet. I'll tell her the police will be here if she wants to talk to them."

My special antennae began waving. Clarice never did anything without a good reason. "I'm going, too," I told her.

So ten minutes later we were walking down the road again. I should have been tired, since we'd been up half the night. But I felt rested and ready to tackle the world. Clarice bounced along beside me, her ugly purse catching the glint of the sun as we hurried along.

Mrs. Coles was surprised to see us, but she was even more surprised when she heard our news. "Edith Quist involved in a scheme like that?" she asked. "I can't believe it . . . Can't believe it!" She continued to gasp and stare over her glasses as we went on with the story.

"So that's why Mr. Brock broke into your store and stole the pictures," Clarice finished.

"The police will be talking to him," I added. "But right now they'll be at our cottage. Aunt Doris has to give the lottery ticket to them. You can go there to talk to them if you want to."

Nervously Mrs. Coles patted the braid wrapped around her head. "Oh no, no. I won't do that. I wouldn't want to do that." She rubbed her hands together and stared at the floor. "So I didn't misplace those pictures after all. They really *were* stolen."

"You knew it all the time," Clarice said, "but you couldn't make a big fuss about them because it would have brought too much attention to those pictures and to you. Especially since you had just written Caroline's name on the back of each of them."

Mrs. Coles gasped. "You know that too?" She glanced at the empty shelf beside her grandfather clock.

"The ink wasn't very old," I explained. "But what I can't figure out is—"

"She wrote that name on those two pictures because she *knew* that little girl was Caroline Merkin, and she suspected something strange was going on," Clarice told me. "She wanted to have us question Mrs. Quist to see why she was so sure that I looked like that girl. She didn't want to create a big fuss herself, but she thought we'd wonder enough to ask some questions."

Clarice pointed to that empty top shelf. "You said you came upon those pictures accidently after you left our cottage, but that wasn't true. I noticed that the dust there was rubbed off in one straight line. That can't happen by accident. The box was purposely, carefully moved forward. You came right here and pulled that box down from the shelf because you knew those pictures were in there."

Mrs. Coles's long face was pale. She turned to look out the window, and I saw that she was twisting her hands together so tightly that the knuckles were white.

"*You're* Caroline Merkin, aren't you?" Clarice whispered.

As her voice died, there was absolute silence. I felt as though someone had just tossed ice water at my face. I heard the ticking of the grandfather clock and the sound of a car passing in the street outside. Mostly though, I heard my own thoughts cartwheeling and bouncing around in my head. Just like you can see hidden animals in those picture puzzles they have for little kids when someone points them out to you, suddenly I could see all the clues showing that Marie Coles was really Caroline Merkin. The girl in the picture had the same dark eyes. She was waving with her left hand, and we knew Mrs. Coles was left-handed. Mrs. Coles truly had hurried back to her shop to pull out those pictures and write her name on the back so that we would wonder why Mrs. Quist was so sure Clarice looked like Caroline Merkin. Then she had pretended that she had mislaid them even though she knew they were stolen.

"How long have you known?" she asked.

"I've only been sure since last night," Clarice said. "All that business with the lottery ticket got me all confused. But finally, when that story was clear, your story became clear, too. I wondered from the start, though, why you dressed so old, acted so old, too. Mrs. Quist tries to dress young, and I guess I can understand that. But you tried hard to look old, and I wondered why. That first day you said you were sixty-two, but I didn't think so. You looked more like my teacher's age—fifty."

"That's the right age!" I blurted. "Ten-year-old Caroline Merkin has been dead as a doornail for forty years!" Then I felt so stupid I felt my face flush. "Well, that's what people *said,*" I added.

Clarice hugged her purse tighter to her chest. "But all those clues weren't what really made me sure you were Caroline Merkin," she said. "I mean, I looked over all my facts in my notebooks, but they weren't enough. I guess sometimes you can know something without logic. I just felt for sure that you were Caroline Merkin because of the way you acted whenever Mr. Merkin's name was mentioned. Your face got all tight and strange."

Mrs. Coles stood up. She moved over and looked out the window. "He was a cruel man. Crueler to me and my mother than you could ever know. She arranged that boating accident, and then she found someone to 'kidnap' me. We went to Europe and lived there for years. I married there. Now that both my mother and my husband are dead, I decided to come back here. I'm not sure I want to see Ezra Merkin again, not sure if I'm ready. But I wanted to be close to the place I lived as a child. Magic Lake is beautiful. I had almost forgotten how beautiful it is here."

Wishing I could think of something wise to say, I stood there curling my toes against my sandal soles. I thought of my own dad, so fun and so gentle, and I couldn't imagine living with someone like Ezra Merkin.

Mrs. Coles turned to look at us again. She cleared her throat. "Well, I guess the story is out now. I truly did think my antique shop would work and my masquerade would keep my secret. But I guess everybody will know it now."

"Nobody else has guessed your secret," Clarice said. "Flee Jay and I won't tell anybody if you don't want us to."

She looked so relieved that I touched her arm, hoping to reassure her even more. "Mr. Brock has the pictures, but he never guessed it was you. It's funny, too, because the story he told us was almost the truth. But he thought he was just making it up."

"I never knew him as a child," Mrs. Coles said. "But don't you think he might suspect after he's had more time to think?"

"He's got lots of other things to think about right now," Clarice said. "He won't be thinking about you or Caroline Merkin at all."

"You won't have to tell anybody unless you want to," I added.

She smiled, and for the first time I saw that she was a pretty woman who had tried to make herself look old and plain. She glanced out the window again. Far off in the distance we could see the hazy outlines of the treetops of Merkin Island.

"Who knows," she said. "I may change my mind and see

my father one day. They say time heals all wounds. And I guess I am a bit curious about him. But I'll wait until I'm ready."

"Will you want to talk to Aunt Doris or the police about the break-in?" I asked.

She shook her head. "No. Let's just forget about that. Mr. Brock didn't harm anything of value. And I have lots of other pictures. I won't make a complaint."

"Maybe nobody will," I said as I stood up to leave. "Then Mrs. Quist won't be in any trouble at all."

Mrs. Coles was still calling thanks to us as we left the store. "I'm glad we promised to keep her secret," I said.

Clarice nodded. "Me too. And I'll bet she goes to see her father eventually."

"Me too," I said. "But just in case he's not pleased to see her, I hope she doesn't arrive while he's having his after-dinner coffee!"

The Decision

As we walked along the road back to the cottage, I felt warm and happy in the bright sunshine. We still had two days left for sunbathing—I could still get tanned and gorgeous. I was in such good spirits, I wanted everyone to feel the same way I felt. "I liked Mrs. Coles, didn't you?" I said to Clarice. "She had lots of sadness in her life, but I think she's going to be happy now. Don't you?"

Clarice shrugged. "You're the one who knows all about emotions, Flee Jay. I only know facts."

"Ha!" I nudged her. "Didn't you just admit back there in the store that you didn't use facts to figure out that Mrs. Coles was really Caroline Merkin?"

She giggled. "I only said that to make you feel good, Flee Jay. I saw how shocked you were when I said I knew about Mrs. Coles, and I knew you didn't have any facts. So I pretended that emotions might be enough. Face it, Sister, without me to keep the facts straight, you and your emotions would be lost. I'm the one who solved this case because I'm the one who has all the brains!"

I reached over to bop her one, but she ran ahead. "Nanny, nanny, boo, boo," she called back. "You can't do what I do!"

* * *

So that's the whole story of the lost lookalike. Do you think Clarice should get all the credit for solving this case?

Neither do I. And I'm making sure I'm ever ready and alert to find the answers to any future cases we might have. So "Nanny, nanny, boo, boo, Clarice. I *can* do what you do!"

From Felice Jennifer Saylor
Girl Detective